CABS, CAKES, AND CORPSES

Murder on the Equator, Book 1

BECCA BLOOM

"Cabs, Cakes, and Corpses: A Jessica James Cozy Mystery"
"Murder on the Equator, Book 1"

All rights reserved. No part of this book may be reproduced in any form or by any electronic or mechanical means including information storage and retrieval systems — except in the case of brief quotations embodied in critical articles or reviews — without permission in writing from its publisher, Becca Bloom.

This is a work of fiction. The characters, locations, and events portrayed in this book are fictitious or are used fictitiously. Any similarity to real persons, living or dead, is purely coincidental and not intended by the author.

Published by Becca Bloom

Facebook: @BeccaBloomWrites
Twitter: @BeccaBloomWrite
Email: contact@beccabloomwrites.com
Want access to bonus chapters, as well as the latest news about my books? Sign up for my New Release Newsletter

Copyright © 2017 Becca Bloom
All rights reserved.
ISBN-13:978-1-944795-95-5

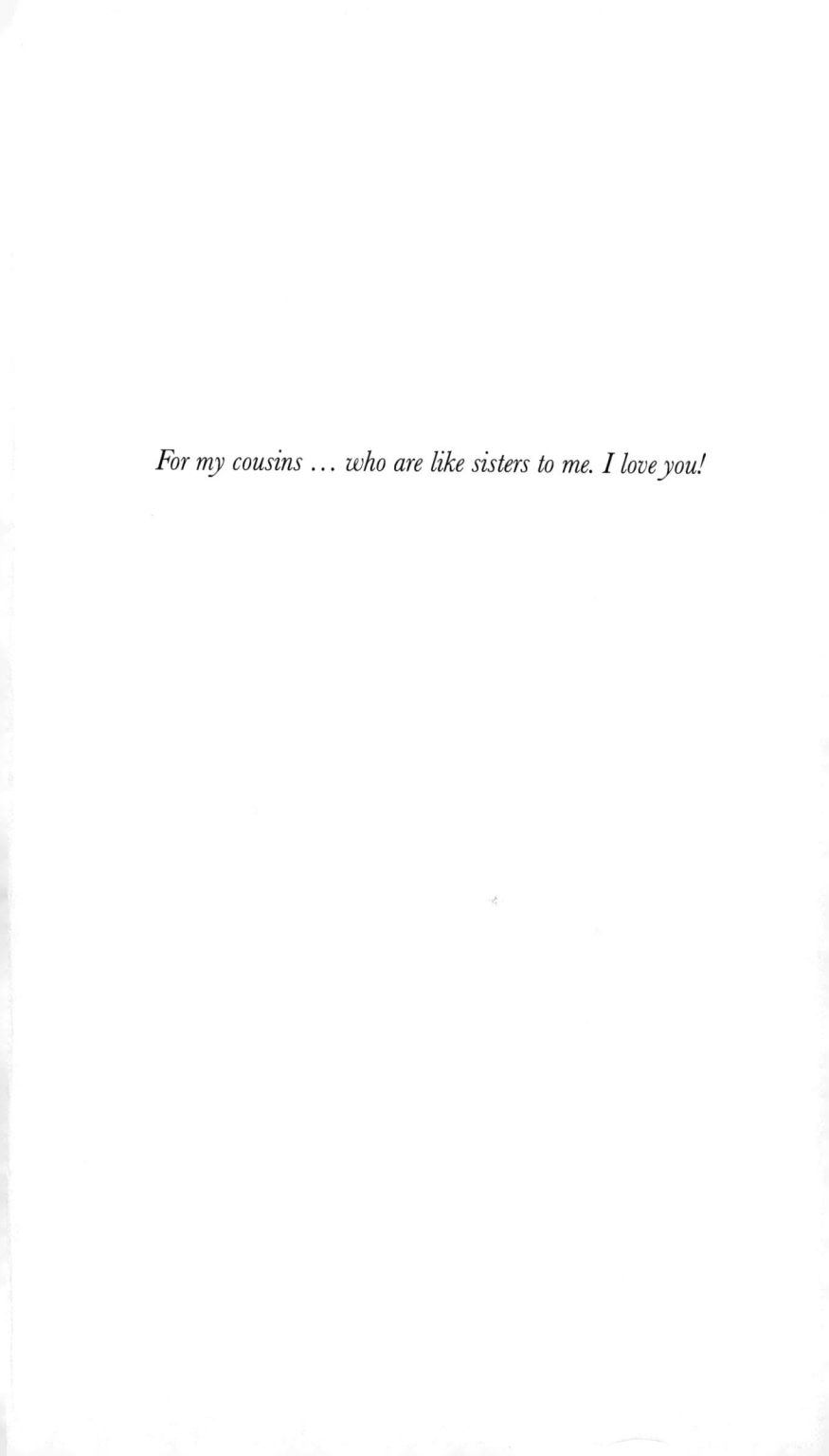

For my cousins ... who are like sisters to me. I love you!

Contents

Chapter 1	1
Chapter 2	11
Chapter 3	22
Chapter 4	37
Chapter 5	50
Chapter 6	65
Chapter 7	76
Chapter 8	89
Chapter 9	97
Chapter 10	108
Chapter 11	117
Chapter 12	125
Chapter 13	133
Chapter 14	142
Chapter 15	150
Chapter 16	160
Chapter 17	170
Chapter 18	177
Chapter 19	185
Chapter 20	195
Chapter 21	206
Chapter 22	216
Chapter 23	225
Chapter 24	232
Chapter 25	240
Chapter 26	250

Thank you!	259
Seco de Pollo	261
Mammy's Goofballs	265
About the Author	267
Other Books by Becca Bloom	269

Chapter 1

"You have got to be kidding me!" I exclaimed. "I'm certain I can identify my own bag." For goodness' sake, I'd had the same leather-bottomed, JanSport backpack with the Kermit the Frog key chain dangling from the zipper of the front pocket since my freshman year of high school. I was not about to let some gum-smacking kleptomaniac with an annoyingly perfect topknot purloin my favorite backpack. Especially when it still had my e-reader inside. I would not survive a month in the jungle without my books.

The airport security agent, clearly bored, could not have cared less about my predicament. He extended his pudgy hand out to the thief, who hugged my bag closer to her. It probably reeked of her cheap perfume by now.

"This woman is crazy. The bag is mine. See? I

even have a tattoo of Kermit." The heister unbuttoned her jeans and pulled them down far enough to reveal the lovable green frog sitting on top of her hip bone in the exact pose on my key chain. "See?" she insisted.

Seriously, what were the odds?

The agent dropped his hand, clearly taking the reprobate's side, after which she gladly handed the bag over, knowing she'd get it back. Just another tragedy in my growing list of reasons why I never want to travel on an airplane again. Ever.

I glared at the gloating delinquent before me. My self-respect would not allow me to go down without a fight. Pushing the handle of my carry-on down with a resounding click I wished was much louder than it was, I crossed my arms and lifted my chin. "Can she itemize every item in my bag?" Pulling out from my pocket the numbered list Jessenia had made me write, I waved it in front of the man.

The bored agent scoffed because, you know, he must have had way more important things to do than deal with me and the crazy scamp who had branded a cheap imitation of my key chain on her hip. Fortunately for me, my voice carried through the square, windowless, gray room in the special part of the Miami airport reserved for confrontational customers.

A big guy who looked like he belonged on a football field came over, taking the list I offered from my hands. His name badge identified him as a supervisor. Thank goodness! Maybe he'd be more reasonable than the balding, rotund agent still staring at the vexing villain's exposed hip. As if the little thief had conveniently forgotten how to zip her pants up.

"What's going on here?" the giant said in a booming voice, perusing the paper in his hand.

The security agent jutted his thumb at me. "This woman claims that this nice lady attempted to steal her backpack."

What? All of a sudden I'm the criminal spouting false charges against sweet, innocent travelers?

Smacking the gum with her mouth open like a cow, the "nice lady" rolled her eyes and said, "Can I have my bag back now? This is so annoying and such a waste of time."

She was annoyed? It took effort, but I was polite. "Please, I just want my stuff back. This has been the worst trip ever and I'm too close to my destination to give up now. I've been randomly selected for additional screening in front of onlooking passengers for flights that were later canceled. I've been waiting almost twenty-four hours in this airport because of thunderstorms. I'm tired, and I run the risk of losing my final flight unless I can get back to my gate in…" I pulled the cell phone out of the pocket of my wrinkled 501s and checked the time. "… Great. I have ten minutes before I miss my flight and so help me, if I have to get on that airplane without the doctor prescribed panic pills in my backpack, I just might do something desperate."

Now, normally, I'm a "go-with-the-flow" kind of

person with a severe allergy to confrontation, but adrenaline had taken over my body and I even scared myself. I must have scared the security agent too. He took a step away from me and toward his supervisor. Wimp.

Big Guy had the audacity to smile. I wasn't joking. He must have known it too. He had my list.

He asked me one question. "What are you reading on your Kindle?"

"I'm forty-eight percent through War and Peace." Appropriate, huh?

"Do I have your permission to get the Kindle out of your bag for confirmation?"

The pilferer crossed her arms and looked up into the corner of the room. I could smell her gum with each smack of her open mouth. Cinnamon. It better not be a stick of my Big Red from the front pocket of my backpack which had been my pillow for the past day of restless naps in the uncomfortable airport chairs. As if I wouldn't notice when someone yanked it out from under my head.

I nodded my consent. If I missed this last flight, that was it. I had endured public humiliation when a TSA officer had selected me out of a line of hundreds for a public pat down. I had then waited an hour as they scanned my carry-on and backpack five times only to discover that the suspicious article they saw in my bag was my reading glasses.

Miami had been no kinder to me. What was

supposed to be a two-hour layover had turned into a twenty-two-hour holdup ... one from which I was about to free myself when the ingrate with designer sunglasses on decided she liked my Kermit the Frog key chain.

I glared at the nefarious nuisance, wishing my eyes had lasers.

The supervisor flipped the screen of my Kindle around for both of us to see. There it was. War and Peace.

Dumping my Kindle back in my bag, he said, "You'd better run, Miss James. I'll radio your gate, but your flight has been delayed so long, it'd cause a mutiny to ask the other passengers to wait any longer."

Looping my arm through my bag and hefting it onto my back, I took his advice and ran. I hoped they threw whoever that skinny tart was into airport jail or something. Or maybe they could seal her in a room with one cramped bathroom that was always busy and give her nothing but bags of salty pretzels and one half-filled glass of water to drink. Oh wait, that was me on my last flight.

My carry-on bumped into the backs of my Converse a few times, but I didn't stop to nurse my injured feet. There was no time.

Sweat trickled down my face and back as I ran the length of Concourse D, weaving through travelers standing in the middle of the wide walkway. My legs and lungs screamed at me, but I saw the bag checker holding the door open, looking around before she would close it.

"Wait! I'm here!"

She smiled at me with her perfectly ironed uniform and smooth French roll, reminding me of how I hadn't had a shower in almost two days. I felt gross, and I'm sure I looked it too.

"Are you Jessica James?" she asked politely.

"Yes. Is the plane still here?"

"It is, but it's a completely booked flight and the overhead bin space is full. You'll have to check your carry-on."

"Is there time for that?"

She went to the desk opposite us and pushed a button. A long baggage ticket printed off and she stuck it around the handle of my bag in a matter of seconds.

"It'll get to Quito when I do?" I asked. I only had the one bag. My laptop, a month's worth of clothes, toiletries, malaria pills, snacks, and sunscreen to protect my pasty white skin was inside. If it got lost ... well, I guess if it got lost, it would be an appropriate ending to this nightmare of a trip my family had so kindly insisted I take. Some gift!

"I'll send it down right now." She waved me through the door and down the ramp to the plane taking me closer to my final destination. Baños, Ecuador. That's right. I was going to spend a month in a place named after a toilet. My dad assured me it's a lovely place, but after the torture I'd been through to get this far, he'd have to forgive me for being skeptical and a touch snarky. I needed a cupcake and a strong cup of coffee.

The flight attendants hustled me down the narrow row, pushing past elbows and wide shoulders. I felt hundreds of eyes glowering at me, and my cheeks burned from their unspoken criticism and my sheer exhaustion. All I wanted to do was sleep. Finally, we reached the second to last row and the only vacant seat on the entire plane.

I fumbled for my boarding pass, hoping there was some mistake.

The flight attendant, another immaculately groomed woman who was losing patience with me, bared her white teeth in a pinched smile. "Please take your seat so we can depart."

The cologne-drenched guy with the slicked back hair in the aisle seat leaned back an eighth of an inch to make my crawl over him all the more enjoyable. The large man in the window seat, who leaned over my middle space, didn't even bother to shift his weight. I practically had to sit on his shoulder to shimmy into my seat. I could feel his breath on my ear. Clutching my backpack to me, I debated if I should offer him a stick of gum or not.

The uptight attendant, her voice strained through her fake smile, said, "Ma'am, please place your carry-on item under the seat in front of you for takeoff."

There was no room to move, and I didn't much like being called "ma'am." Goodness' sake alive, I was only twenty-three. No older than the flight attendant appeared to be. Sliding my bag between my legs and down to the floor, I pushed it under the seat in front of me gently with my foot, trying to keep my shoe on the strap so I could attempt to retrieve it again.

I closed my eyes, imagined myself reading by a cozy fire in my dream cottage by the sea, and began counting my breaths. The plane shook and my stomach dropped to the floor as we took off.

"Hey, lady, you okay?" asked Cologne Man to my right, with a thick Latino accent.

I cracked my eyes open.

He pulled a bag up from down by his feet with an ease which made me a bit jealous. The clinking of glass inside the large, plastic bag from the duty free store gave me an image of giant bottles of perfume. My guess was close.

"You want a drink?" he asked, pulling the plastic down so I could see the full-sized bottles of Johnny Walker whiskey, Smirnoff vodka, and Antioqueño aguardiente.

I looked back up at him. Was he joking?

"No, thank you."

He seemed disappointed, so I added. "It was nice of you to offer, though."

That earned a toothy smile and he extended his hand out for me to shake. "My name is José Guzmán."

I shook his hand. "I'm Jessica." I kept it short and

polite in the hopes he wouldn't turn out to be the chatty sort who wouldn't let me read or nap.

"I visit my family in Miami. You know Miami?" he asked.

"I've never been." Okay, that's enough chat.

"I am from Baños. Is beautiful place. Many tourist go there. You visit Baños?" José gently wrapped a roll of bubble wrap around the bottles and put them back under the seat.

I wasn't about to tell all my travel plans to a stranger. "I'm sure I'll make it there."

"Okay. I look for you! I show you good bars."

I was spared from having to give an answer when the seatbelt light turned off. He pulled out one of those round wrap-around neck rests, the latest iPhone, placed Skullcandy headphones over his ears, and reclined his seat.

The guy on my left still leaned over my space, but José's cologne was giving me a headache and I needed to distance myself. I nestled into my cramped spot as well as I could and felt my body relax and drift off into delicious slumber... until something slammed against the back of my seat, hurling me forward. Big guy felt it too and moved his weight over to the window.

Turning around, I saw a little blonde girl with a sticky face and a juice box in her hands. She met my eyes and, with a diabolical giggle, kicked my seat again. I looked over to her mother who frantically rocked her screaming infant in a desperate attempt to shush him. She reached over to stop her daughter from kicking my seat again and looked at me apologetically. "I'm so sorry. They should sleep soon."

They didn't sleep. Not for even one minute of the four-hour flight.

Chapter 2

Why was I traveling by myself to a foreign country in South America where I knew nobody and couldn't speak the language? To be fair, I could be polite, order a beer, and ask where the bathroom was (kind of pointless in a town named Baños), but that was pretty much it. So, why? Really, really good question and one I had ample time to ponder during the long, sleepless flight.

Short answer: My family conspired against me. They staged an intervention where they pointed out what they thought was a big issue, namely, that they had all celebrated grand success in their dream lives recently and were moving on to new and exciting things. Being the caring, lovable bunch they are, they felt bad for leaving me behind in Portland, Oregon with my secure, but drab, job.

My oldest sister, Jessenia, was pregnant with her second child. She was moving up to Washington to support her husband's construction company while single-handedly managing her own booming online organization business and teaching her first son, Jayden, how to read at the age of two. I wished she would stick to organizing other peoples' lives and leave me alone sometimes, but what were older sisters for if not to boss their younger sisters around?

My youngest sister, Jessamyn, had been accepted into a highly-coveted modeling agency internship in New York. She was the gorgeous, free spirit of our family. And the one most likely to call me for a loan when she'd maxed out her credit card on a designer dress or tickets to Rome when her rent was due.

My mom was going to be featured in September's edition of Digital Photographer in a spread on award-winning photos. She was the CEO of her own studio and the most talented photographer I knew.

Dad had finished a sculpture he had been working on for over a year. Buyers had lined up for it, and to celebrate, he and Mom had bought an RV. They planned to chase inspiration all over the country for the next six months while Mammy, my dad's mom and my favorite person in the whole world, house-sat their home in the Portland suburbs.

They pitied my simple life designing webpages and other graphic artsy things in the solitude of my cozy, studio apartment in the Pearl District of Portland. They thought I needed a grand adventure.

Lost in my thoughts, I hardly noticed when the plane landed. The applause of the passengers jolted me back to reality. I pulled out my phone, checking for messages. My flight delay had messed up the plans of the Jimenez family to pick me up, but Sylvia assured me that someone would be there for me. All I had to do was look for a sign with my name on it. Sylvia's straight-forward, precise way of writing reminded me so much of my mom, my relief was real. I'd heard horror stories about the buses in Ecuador and was grateful for her help.

"You have ride?" asked José. "My wife drive taxi."

I was so ready to get outside after having spent hours breathing in the same circulated, perfume-infested air. I didn't think I could stand another four hours to Baños. "I'm all set. Thank you. Have a safe trip to your home."

We shook hands and parted ways as the crowds disembarking from three arriving flights that afternoon merged in a jumbled mass in the hallway leading to immigration.

Not having any luggage to slow me down, I looped my arms through my backpack and made good progress skirting along the edge of the walkway. However, halfway to the little booths where I would get my first stamp in my passport, I had to stop to catch my breath before continuing my trudge through the masses. Either I was in worse physical shape than I had thought or I had underestimated the effects of Quito's high elevation. Oxygen was in scant supply at eight thousand feet. People shouldn't live this high, my lungs screamed as I wrestled through the crowded hallway only to wait an eternity in the immigration line.

First, there was the line for the stamp in my passport. Then there was a line to get my bag. Then there was another line where they insisted on riffling through my bag. As if I hadn't been through enough security in the past two days. Finally, there was a line jammed up by overflowing luggage carts and unruly kids just to get out of the sliding glass doors leading out of the airport.

Tired, hungry, and wanting — no, needing! — a shower, I scanned the crowd for a sign with my name written on it, knowing that I wore a scowl. So help me, if my ride out of here was late, I would change my ticket for the first flight back home. After I managed to get a shower, that was. And a doughnut with lots of frosting.

Finally, I saw it. A woman with dark eyes and bronze hair smiled at me as I lugged my bag over to her.

"Señorita Jessica?" she asked.

"Yes. Thank goodness you're here! It's been a long day."

She smiled and nodded at me, reaching to help me with my bag. Turning around, she took off through the crowd.

"Oh, I guess I'll follow you then," I said, trying my best to keep up with her without bumping into too many people on our way outside.

The pocket of her Aeropostale sweatshirt rang,

and she deposited my carry-on in the trunk of a yellow taxi before answering it. With a smile and the universally understood sign of pinching her fingers together to communicate that I give her a moment, she answered.

I understood nothing and was terrified when she held the phone out to me. When I hesitated, she pushed it toward me, saying, "You speak." At least, I think that's what she said.

Taking the phone, I said, "Hello?"

"Jessica?" said a woman's voice on the other end.

"Yes?" I answered slowly. Please, please, please speak English…

"Hi! This is Sylvia. We're thrilled you're coming to visit us. Your parents are such dear friends of ours. I'm so sorry my son couldn't pick you up, but he had a jungle tour scheduled today, so I arranged for Maria to drive you here. Her husband came in on the same flight. Isn't that convenient?"

She spoke quicker than I could reply, but eventually, she had to breathe. "Thank you for arranging for transportation," I said, before she could start in again.

"Think nothing of it! Maria will drive you straight to my restaurant. You'll stay with my daughter, Adriana, in the apartment above it. I sent some food with her because there aren't many places along the way to stop. Please help yourself and we look forward to seeing you in about four hours! If you need anything, don't hesitate to call me or ask Maria's husband, José. He speaks English."

Cologne Dude. Lovely. "I think I'm good. Thank you."

I heard something like the sound of plates crashing. "Ay, caramba! I have to go. See you in a bit!" The phone beeped in my ear.

Handing it back to Maria, I said, "Gracias."

As promised, there was a cooler. I opened it and was delighted to see a sandwich, a bottle of orange Fanta, and a packet of Oreo cookies inside. Just like the lunches Mammy had packed me for school (except she would never send "pagan" cookies with me when she always had homemade goodies on hand). When I was little, I dreamt of opening a bakery so I could spend all day with her eating yummy treats.

José showed up then, pushing a luggage cart with four giant duffel bags on it. I looked between them and the trunk. Nope. There's no way they'd fit.

"Hi, Jessica!" he waved as if I were a long-lost friend.

"Hey," I raised my hand to wave, nearly pushing him away from me when he leaned forward to kiss me on the cheek.

"Is how we greet here," he laughed along with Maria. "You get used to it."

He hugged his wife, but she was more interested in the duty free bag he carried than in his public display of affection. Pulling the bottles out one by one and turning them around in her hands, she jumped up and down, squealing and speaking a million words a minute. Only then did she act like she was happy to see José.

He explained to me, "She like the whiskey. Is gift from me to my wife."

An odd gift, to be sure, but she was obviously pleased with it, so who was I to judge? So long as she didn't drink any of it on the drive home.

The next few minutes were spent trying to squeeze all of our luggage into the trunk of the car. Two fit, leaving the other two in the backseat with me and my carry-on which was squished behind the driver's seat on the floorboard. I'd have to hold Sylvia's cooler on my lap. I almost forgot about my backpack until I tried to sit down with it still on my back.

Seeing my problem, José reached out to take my bag from me. "I put it in trunk. It safe."

I thought about it. All of my important travel documents, my money, and my cell phone were spread out between the pockets of my jeans and sweater. My laptop was protected inside a case, inside a padded daypack, inside my carry-on. Hey, I don't take chances with my hardware.

The only item of value in my backpack was my e-reader. However, I hadn't come all this way to bury my nose in my Kindle when there were volcanoes to see. My mom would expect pictures.

Handing him my backpack, I twisted around to see him tuck it into one corner of the trunk. It took him three attempts to shut the trunk over the duffel bags bulging out, but he eventually got it. Hopping into the front seat, we took off to the sound of 80s music playing on the radio.

Maria looked at me in her rearview mirror. "You like English music? I learning." She smacked José's hand when he reached for the radio tuner.

"Yes, thank you," I said as I pulled the pop out of the cooler to the tune of Bananarama singing about the cruelties of summer.

Untwisting the Fanta lid slowly, and hearing it hiss, I raised the bottle to my lips just as Maria stepped on the gas. Shrieking as the cold beverage spilled down the front of my shirt, she slammed on the brakes and looked back at me.

"You okay, miss?" she asked.

Not really, but nothing would be okay until I got a shower. I dabbed my sticky, stained shirt with the napkins Sylvia had packed in the cooler and tried to smile. "I'm okay. Thank you."

Maria, as I learned to appreciate during the four-hour blood-curdling drive to Baños, only knew two speeds. Petal to the metal and stop — each of which she did as abruptly as a Formula One racer speeding into or out of a pit stop. José provided the occasional distraction by pointing out the volcanoes we sped by on the Pan American Highway.

"Some people, they call this Volcano Alley."

"Are any of them active?" I asked, confident that with the series of unfortunate events during my travels, at least one of them would be.

"For now? Only Cotopaxi and Tungurahua. We

see Cotopaxi soon." He pointed to the left of the car. The wall of luggage wouldn't let me see anything out of that side.

"Oh," he said, understanding my predicament. "No matter. You definitely see Tungurahua. You know, it mean Throat of Fire in Quechua. Baños location at base of Tungurahua."

"Baños is at the bottom of an active volcano?" How did I not know this before? Jessenia had me so busy with her incessant list-making, and I'd had to rush to finish my outstanding contracts before I left, I'd trusted Mom and Dad to provide me with all the information I had needed. Clearly, I was way too trusting if they thought staying in a town at the bottom of an exploding volcano was something I'd enjoy.

José didn't seem bothered by it. He chuckled as if my question wasn't one hundred percent serious.

"Is Baños safe from the volcano?" I swallowed hard.

José twisted back to face me, his face excited. "We drive by lava path from last big boom! Is close to town!"

Well, that was comforting. Fortunately — or unfortunately, it depended how you looked at it — Maria took all worries of death by exploding volcanoes out of my mind when she swerved to the left and José's bags pinned me against the door.

I also learned that red lights were more of a suggestion than a requirement. Pedestrians most definitely did not have the right of way, as they crossed the highway lane by lane through flowing traffic. Oh, and seat-belts were considered a luxury — one which Maria's fancy car could not boast. I contented myself by wedging my feet against the bottom of José's seat and locking my door.

I never did see Cotopaxi, but I did see the rugged, twin peaks of an inactive volcano José identified to me as the Illinizas. They looked like an old married couple. The man's hair was white with snow and his wife had a touch of white at her temples (which she would no doubt cover at her next appointment with her hairdresser).

Tapping José on the shoulder and interrupting the zombie shooting game he played on his iPad, I asked him about them.

"Illiniza Sur is humid. Is why it has snow and glacier. Illiniza Norte is dry. They are protected in Ecological Reserve," he said hurriedly without looking up.

I contorted my body to extract my phone from my jeans pocket. I wished the photo could express the contrast between the two giants.

Tungurahua came into view three silent, long hours later as we neared a city called Ambato.

Maria, who had not spoken since the outskirts of Quito — not even to her husband — pointed to the giant volcano. "We arrive Baños less hour."

José translated, "She say we arrive to Baños in less than hour."

Cabs, Cakes, and Corpses

That got Maria talking. I could only guess she was mad at him for translating her English when I had understood her just fine. The tongue-lashing José received left no doubt in my mind as to who the boss was in that family. When he tried to ignore her, she smacked the iPad out of his hands.

I ignored the ensuing brawl between the loving couple to appreciate the active volcano I would be living at the base of for a month. It didn't look too scary from here. Half of it was dusted with snow, but the other half broke off into a jagged crater. It reminded me of the Batman villain, Two-Face. Raising my camera, I clicked between the enthusiastic gestures exchanged between the occupants of the front seat just as a puff of black smoke rose from the ugly side of the volcano. My heart leapt up into my throat and I couldn't have breathed had I remembered how.

Chapter 3

Interrupting the irate verbal battle going on in the front seat, I slapped José on the shoulder and pointed. The dark cloud rose, pushing its way through the puffy, white clouds like a bully. "Is that normal?" I squeaked.

The bickering stopped long enough for him to dismiss my concern with a casual wave of his hand. "It happen all the time. No big deal."

"You're sure?" I insisted. It didn't look like no big deal to me. It looked like ash.

"You think we live in Baños if it not safe? We not stupid," he snapped, speaking to me in the same tone he used on his equally incensed wife.

Whatever. I left them to continue their verbal assault against each other and watched the volcano. Was it a prophetic symbol of how my vacation would be?

Why was I here anyway? I patted around my coat pockets until I heard the crinkle of the paper I searched for. Pulling out the first sheet my fingers touched, I heard Mammy's voice in my head as I re-read her letter.

DEAREST JESS,

I'll have to keep myself busy while you're gone or I'll miss you too much. Don't tell your sisters, but you've always been my favorite grandchild.

You know it was your mother, Lord love her, who planned this 'grand adventure.' She did it because she loves you and she doesn't understand that not everyone feels the need to change the world and leave their mark as she and your sisters do.

You're just like your father. He finds happiness in the smaller details of life. For his sake, I'm thrilled you agreed to this trip. The guilt he feels because of how you were affected when his twin disappeared... I still can't think about it without feeling a tremendous loss. Just like him, I don't suppose I'll ever accept it. But we all agree that you suffered the most. This is our attempt to make it better. You take care of everyone, sweet pea. Now, it's time for you to have some fun. Act like the young, beautiful girl you are.

I included some of my best recipes in case you need a taste of home. From what I hear, you'll need them.

Now, I'd better get going or I'll be late for my hip hop dance class. I'm finally getting the hang of the pop and lock.

I love you, honey,

Mammy

I PUT Mammy's letter back with the rest and patted my pocket, trying not to think of the day Dad got the phone call. I had been home with him, being too little for school and too old to want to go with my mom and baby sister to the boring grocery store when I could stay home and watch Pinky and the Brain with my dad. I'm glad he hadn't been alone.

Shrugging off my melancholy, I looked out the window I was squished against. The climate grew warmer and the vegetation thicker as we drove down the mountains. I peeled off my coat and put it inside the empty cooler on my lap. My eyelids drooped under the weight of exhaustion and my head bobbed before I rested it against the soft pillow of a duffel bag.

I WOKE WITH A START, flinging my arms out blindly. My nose smashed against the back of José's seat as I rammed into it. Maria flung her door open, charging the few steps to the intersection blocked by a beat up taxi. Horns honked all around us and voices shouted.

Where were we?

José pulled his bags onto the sidewalk and pried

my squished carry-on out from the backseat. "Welcome to Baños!" He opened his arms and waved them around him.

My vision was still blurry with sleep and the knock to the head I'd taken. Cooler in tow, I climbed out of the car to stand by my bag.

Maria was in a shouting match with the taxi driver blocking the one-way street. He had a badly done tiger tattoo on his forearm. I doubted any man would want his tough tiger to look more like the Pink Panther.

A tall, lanky dude wearing a white undershirt and thick, gold chain joined Bad Tat Man. José frowned at the scene.

"What's going on?" I asked through my daze.

"Christian is looking for trouble. Nobody win against Maria." José sounded like he spoke from experience.

José shoved his bags back into the car and shouted for Maria to join him.

Still a bit disoriented, I asked, "Are we at Sylvia's?"

We were parked in a narrow street. On one side was a park bursting with bougainvillea, puffy trees with curly leaves and red blossoms, giant palm trees, and all sorts of colorful flowers.

On the side of the walk we stood on was a row of businesses selling alpaca teddy bears, brightly woven purses and hammocks, ice cream, and food. The warm breeze smelled like sweet pineapple. Or maybe that was the orange Fanta I'd spilled on my shirt.

"Is here," he pointed to the two-story building with a red and white striped awning under a painted sign which read, Abuelita's Kitchen. He yelled again at Maria, and when she showed no signs of budging, he pulled her away, practically pushing her into the car.

Maria honked her horn at the battered taxi blocking our way, adding to the loud melee and making my head pound at the noise. As if she hadn't needed to stop in the middle of the street to let me out anyway. I held onto my carry-on with one hand and tried to cover at least one ear with the other.

The beaten up taxi took off with both of the men inside, its trunk popping open and a plastic bag flying out of it. Oh, my backpack was still in Maria's trunk!

Maria and José didn't hear me shout for them to stop over the noise of passing tourists and honking horns. Gunning the engine, Maria lurched forward and sped away.

A sick feeling made my ears ring. My e-reader and bullet journal had been in my backpack.

I stood in the middle of the sidewalk, with a death grip on my suitcase, not even caring when passersby bumped into me or the cooler at my feet. I was hot and sweaty, my shirt was sticky, and I was stuck in a country I wasn't convinced I wanted to be in. This vacation hated me.

Feeling as if I had made the worst mistake of my

life by agreeing to come here, and wondering why my parents had ever thought this was a good idea, I turned toward the restaurant to see a supermodel looking at me with her mouth open. Great. As if I didn't feel awkward already. Let the beautiful people stare at me when I knew I looked a fright. I tucked a chunk of my stringy blonde hair behind my ear as I bent over to pick up the cooler.

Best get this over with. Rolling my carry-on under the shady, striped awning, I said, "Hi, I'm Jessica. Is this the Jimenez residence? I'm supposed to meet Sylvia here."

"Oh my gosh, you're finally here! What happened? You look like you've just been mugged or had your dog run over." With that, her eyes widened. "Don't tell me Maria ran over someone! She promised she'd be careful. She's usually a pretty good driver."

I struggled to push my bag forward. "No, she didn't run over anyone, but she drove off with my backpack still in her trunk."

She gasped. "Oh, no! Did you have anything important in it?"

"Aside from my journal and my e-reader, not really," I said, not wanting to start off our acquaintance by revealing what a weirdo I was if I told her I'd rather have lost my money belt than those two treasured possessions.

"I'll give her a call and ask if she can drop your knapsack off here as soon as she can." She reached out to take the cooler from my arms. "I'm Adriana

Jimenez. My friends call me Adi. Sylvia is my mother. Let me help you with that." She pushed the plastic handle of my suitcase down and leaned forward to kiss me on the cheek.

I stood there as stiff as a board, unaccustomed to the invasion of my personal space.

Adriana laughed. "You'll get used to it. We greet with a kiss on the cheek here. Are you hungry or do you want a shower first?"

It was like she had read my mind. "A shower would be nice."

She lifted my bag like it weighed nothing. Beautiful, skinny, and deceptively strong.

Bright tapestries adorned the sunshine yellow wall to my left. Large, wood-framed windows at the front and to my right flooded sunlight over the pine tables and upholstered chairs in bold color combinations matching the tapestries on the walls and the runners down the tables. Twinkle lights dangled from exposed beams above our heads.

We passed a reception area which also housed bottles of wine and a few assorted liquors. I followed Adriana through a swinging door into the kitchen.

The first thing I noticed was the butcher block island with aquamarine legs and gleaming stainless steel pots and pans dangling above it. Bar stools tucked under the large counter surface surrounded it. The refrigerator hummed next to me.

To my left was an industrial-sized stove surrounded by pine cabinets and white counters and manned by an elegant woman with sleek, black hair pulled into a perfect chignon.

Setting my bag down, Adriana pointed to the classy woman stirring a pot on the stove. "That is my mom, Sylvia. She always said that your mother was her American twin." I could see it. My mom always looked polished and never left the house without lipstick on.

Nodding to the opposite side of the room, where there was an extra stove and a large sink with dirty dishes piled up as high as the window overlooking the street above it, Adriana added in a lower tone, "And that is my grandmother. Bertha is her name, but we all call her Abuelita. Don't look at her too long or she'll notice us. If we're lucky, we'll slip past her unseen." The elderly woman with jet black hair made up for her lack of height with the volume of her voice. She pointed at the pile of dishes and barked orders to a young lady who looked terrified of her.

Against the back wall was a freezer and a table laden with cookbooks stacked next to a coffeemaker, mismatched mugs, and a sugar bowl with a parrot painted on it.

It wasn't difficult for me to guess that the three women were related. They all had smooth, dark hair, thin figures, and high cheekbones.

Sylvia waved us over to join her and hugged me as if she'd known me my entire life and hadn't seen me in ages. "We're so happy you're here!" she said, rocking me back and forth.

With another rock and a back-popping squeeze, she released me and nodded in Abuelita's direction. In a whisper, she said, "She's on the war path today. Tia Rosa decided to join Miss Patty's art class and Mom is mad she's not around to help with the dinner crowd. She's not always like this, but consider yourselves warned."

Adriana added, "Abuelita must be out of Twinkies. She gets grumpy if she hasn't had her daily dose of sugar and carbs."

I could empathize with that. Everyone in my family knew to offer Mammy a gooey treat when she got snappy. Their trick worked fairly well on me, for that matter.

"Who is Tia Rosa?" I asked.

"She is Abuelita's older sister. Tia is the Spanish word for 'aunt.' Without her sister here, Abuelita is tormenting my waitresses. I'm going to have to give them a raise today for putting up with her. I'll take it out of Abuelita's salary," Sylvia added with an impish grin. Wrapping her arm around me, she said, "Enough about my cantankerous mother. It's so good you are here, Jessica. It's been nearly thirty years since I've seen your mother, but I still consider her my best friend."

"Mamita, we need to call the Guzmáns. Jessica's knapsack is in the trunk of Maria's taxi," said Adriana.

"Ay, no! Did you have any valuables in your bag?"

"My e-reader." Only the most valuable of all valuables. Cracked screen and all. And my bullet journal. Oh, and my twin box pack of Big Red gum.

Sylvia raised her arched eyebrows. "I will call her before she picks up any other fares. Hopefully, she decided to call it a day. Why don't you let Adi show you to your room while I call? I don't imagine Maria will be able to return before a half an hour with all the traffic outside. As you may have noticed, most of our streets are one lane and one-way. They get crowded on the weekend."

Sylvia made it sound like it wasn't a big deal. And it wouldn't have been had I not had the only item guaranteed to help me endure a month here taken away from me.

Adriana motioned for me to follow her to the back of the kitchen, where there was a screen door by the coffeemaker leading out to a stone pathway with a small patch of grass with a flower border on the far side.

The property was surrounded by a tall, cement wall. Directly to the right was a concrete washing tank, and above it were some wooden stairs taking us up to Adriana's apartment.

"It gets noisy here on the busy days, but I think you'll be comfortable. I asked Jake to change the gas tank for us before he left yesterday, so you should have hot water for your shower. We hope you'll eat with us downstairs. We use distilled water and soak everything that comes out of the ground, so you shouldn't have problems with parasites or amoebas. Abuelita always makes enough. She thinks it's her mission in life to fatten us up."

I looked down at the denim stretching over my hips. "I don't need any help in that department," I joked.

"You're so lucky!"

Convinced she was just being nice, I mimicked Mammy's famous quote, "Everything I have, I owe to … pastry."

Adriana laughed, shaking her head. "What? Not spaghetti, Sophia Loren? I had forgotten what it's like in developed countries. You all want to look like tall, twelve-year-old boys, but it's different down here. We like women to look like women. Soft, round curves are admired. If you don't believe me, you can ask Jake."

The stairs creaked as we walked up them. Like my apartment in Portland, she had three locks to get through before the door would open.

"Who is Jake?"

"He's my twin brother and the biggest pest in all of Baños." Adriana rolled her eyes with a smile. "He was going to pick you up from Quito, but he had a day trip scheduled with a tour group this morning and wasn't able to get a replacement when we found out your flight was delayed." She checked her watch. "He should be home soon."

"What kind of tours?" I asked, thinking I should act like a tourist while I'm here. I wouldn't mind going back to get some better pictures of the sleepy volcanoes I'd seen outside of Quito. Maybe, then, I could finally see Cotopaxi.

"Mostly adventure tours. You know, things like mountain climbing, white water rafting, zip lining through the jungle like he's Tarzan or something. If you want, he can take you on his next tour. I think it involves bungee jumping."

"No!" I said a bit too enthusiastically as we stepped inside. "I mean, I'm more of a 'keep-my-feet-on-steady-ground' kind of girl. It doesn't sound like something I'd enjoy."

"Nothing wrong with that. I went with him once and that was enough for me. I'm a city girl through and through." She took her sandals off, leaving them on a rug next to the door.

As I unlaced my Converse, I pondered the simplicity of wearing flip flops. The wood floor was warm under my toes.

Adriana opened the first door on the left of the entryway and motioned for me to leave my bag there. "Now, this is your room. Please make yourself comfortable." Bolts of fabric were stacked neatly in a corner and sketches covered the walls. She pointed to the next door on the left. "This is our bathroom. Feel free to use whatever you need there. My room is just across the hall and everything else, I think, is pretty obvious."

The hallway opened up to a living room decorated with turquoise and orange throw pillows to match the geometric design on the rug between the brown leather couch and the shelf used as an entertainment center. Black and white photographs of smiling people and famous European landmarks dressed up the white walls. Behind the couch was a marble counter-top with a dark purple KitchenAid sitting in the middle.

"I need to help out in the kitchen before the dinner customers come. If you need anything, just holler, okay?"

A shower. I desperately needed a shower.

It took me a while to figure out what the F and the C labeling the shower faucets meant, but with the help of my Spanish-English dictionary, I soon had the hot water going. F for frio and cold. C for calor and hot.

I grabbed a fresh change of clothes from my bag and a towel from the shelf above the toilet, testing the temperature of the water with my fingers until it felt perfect. Then, I made sure the long, skinny window at the top of the shower was closed so the room would fill with steam.

I let the hot water beat the kinks out of my shoulders. Lathering my hair with the coconut shampoo I'd found in the shower caddy, I massaged my scalp until my hands filled up with the scented lather. I was just starting to feel human again when the water turned to ice. Screaming as I jumped out of the way, my feet slipped on the wet tiles and I grabbed the first thing within grasp to break my fall — the shower curtain.

The curtain rod gave, smacking me with a resounding clank to my forehead on its descent.

My eyes stung from the shampoo suds running down my face. Someone pounded on the front door, but I was more concerned about shutting off the freezing water.

Crawling forward and reaching toward the spigot blindly, I screamed again when my hand touched warm skin. Skin too warm to belong to me.

Blinking and rubbing at my eyes, I heard a man's voice say, "Stay where you are. I'm turning off the water."

Instinctively, I grabbed at the shower curtain to spread it over myself, trying to remember if it was clear or opaque. Please, please, please let it not be clear.

"Here," he said, holding out a towel.

I took it, wiped my eyes dry, made sure he wasn't looking, then wrapped the towel around me as I got to my feet.

"Are you okay?" he asked, his back still turned away from me.

I heard someone clumping up the stairs. "Gato, is everything—" Adriana froze when she saw me standing in the shower, shampoo dripping down my hair and, from the pulsating ache I felt on my forehead, a growing goose egg front and center on my face.

She visibly struggled not to laugh. "Well, I can see

you two have finally met. Gato, you can turn around. Jess, this is my brother, Jake."

Gato … cat. Why would she call her brother a cat? He turned around and I forgot how to speak, completely mesmerized by the brightest green eyes I had ever seen.

Chapter 4

My eyes were bright red from the soap, my nose was red, and my forehead was swollen. But my clothes were clean and I didn't feel grimy anymore. Fluffing my long hair out so it wouldn't dry flat against my head, I went downstairs to the kitchen, praying all the while that Jake would miraculously disappear and I would never have to see him again. Nor him me. He'd already seen enough.

As soon as the screen door shut behind me, I knew he was in the room. Adriana stifled a laugh.

Sylvia had the grace to look away, but her shoulders shook.

Abuelita walked up to me, smacking a rolling pin against her palm.

"You meet my grandson, eh," she said in an accusatory tone.

My face burned. "You could say that." A self-conscious chuckle escaped me. If you can't beat them, join them. I could appreciate the humor of the situation, and though it was difficult to laugh about it at that moment, I knew it would be much funnier tomorrow. Or the day after. Okay, more like a year later. Still, better to laugh than to cry.

I saw him then, without soap burning my eyes and mortification clouding my view. He walked around the island, a cup of steaming, black coffee in his hand. Abuelita reached up on her tiptoes and patted his cheek while he extended the coffee out to me. He was handsomer now that I could see properly. Six feet plus of chiseled, honey-skinned perfection. And those eyes.

"Welcome to our home," he said. He wore a slight smile, but he did not laugh at me. I looked into his hypnotizing lime green eyes and nearly dropped the mug.

"Thank you," I managed to mumble, running my finger up the side of the cup before the drops of coffee I'd sloshed over the side fell to the floor.

Abuelita strengthened her adoring pats to a smart smack, and she poked one end of the rolling pin into Jake's chest. She was half his height, but that didn't seem to bother her in the least.

"You forget change gas tank!" she charged.

"I'm sorry, Abuelita," he said repentantly. "It won't happen again." His lips curled up clear to the corners of his eyes.

His smile worked like a charm on her, as I imagine it would on any female with a pulse. Retracting her rolling pin, she smiled back, saying, "See it no happen again. You apologize to our guest." She waved her pin toward me, and I jumped back before it connected with my nose. My face had suffered enough hits for the day.

She stuck out her other hand and I instinctively shook it. "My name Bertha. You call me Abuelita," she ordered before glaring at her forgetful grandson.

Jake turned to me, his smile widening enough to show the gap between his front teeth, adding a level of adorable to his already impressive hotness. "I am sorry. Let me make it up to you by showing you around Baños when you're rested up."

Adriana joined in the conversation. "Ay, no! Not one of your boring tours. Take us to The Shamrock! We can dance, and you can buy us drinks!" She wrapped her arm around my shoulders.

Filled with a sense of camaraderie, I said, "That sounds nice. Can we go tomorrow, though? I have a Skype date with my family tonight. They're worried sick after all the problems I had getting here."

"Tomorrow it is! Tia Rosa will cover for me," said Adriana excitedly.

Jake scowled at his sister. "My tours are never boring."

"Dancing and drinks?" she insisted.

He held up his hands in surrender. "Okay, okay. Have your way." To me, he said, "I'll show you around another day."

My knees shook like Jell-O, but I held myself together. "I look forward to it!" I replied like an enthusiastic, teenage tourist. Just shoot me now. I couldn't have acted more like a goober had I tried.

Sylvia stopped chopping. Laying down her knife, she said, "Please give your parents my love."

I pulled out my cell phone to check the time. I'd need to turn it off to save its battery until Maria returned my backpack. The charger had been inside. "I will so long as my phone doesn't die. Were you able to contact Maria?"

"I called as soon as Adi told me about it. Maria answered the phone and said she'd stop by as soon as she could. I'm guessing it might be a few minutes longer. It sounded like José was fighting with his neighbor or something."

Abuelita interrupted, "Drama, drama, drama. That people watch too much soap opera."

I wasn't surprised. "They fought most of the way home, then she got into a yelling match with a couple guys in a beat-up taxi before she raced off."

Jake nodded. "José and Maria are like vinegar and water. Still, they've stuck it out for five years. That's more than what most people can say."

Abuelita jabbed her finger in Jake's arm, "José too scare for to get divorce. He stuck with her until he die and he know it."

Speaking of death… "This waiting is killing me. If you think it might take a while, I'd rather go get my backpack and be done with it." It was five o'clock and my family would call in a couple hours.

They looked at me funny. Finally, Sylvia said,

"Honey, you've come to the wrong place if waiting affects you so badly."

Jake leaned forward and looked at my phone. "I have a charger for that. I'll swing by the office and drop it off here before I head home. That way, if Maria isn't in, you don't have to miss your family's call."

"Thank you," I said, trying not to picture him riding a white horse in shining armor, his hair ruffling in the breeze and his teeth glinting as the heavens poured sunlight over his knightly self.

"You get lost. I go with you," said Abuelita, pulling her apron over her head and putting an end to my entertaining thoughts.

The room went quiet. I didn't know where Maria's house was, so I obviously needed someone to go with me. I just wasn't sure how I felt about Abuelita being the one to volunteer. She scared me a little.

She charged out of the room, stopping at the swinging door. "You come or what?"

Hastening over to her, I followed as she marched through the restaurant and out to the sidewalk.

"Does Maria live close?" I asked.

"She live on other side of town."

"Should we get a taxi?"

"We walk."

"It is not far, then?" I hadn't had time to change out of my flip flops and didn't know if my toes could handle anything more than a few blocks.

"Baños small town."

Okay then. Her curt answers didn't encourage conversation, but it felt awkward walking beside her as she marched down the road. People moved out of her way to bump into me as we passed.

Without the distraction of conversation, I took the opportunity to look around. Baños really was a charming town, nestled between verdant mountains and a river at the bottom of the ravine. Every house had a garden, and the air smelled sweet with flower blossoms and something more potent. Not flower sweet. I looked around and found a man pulling taffy with his hands, stretching it out and slapping it against the wood door frame where he wrapped it around a peg to pull again. He ripped off a piece and offered it to me.

"Toma," he said.

"You take," Abuelita translated, pausing only long enough to toss the words over her shoulder.

"For you," he added, when I hesitated.

"Gracias," I said to the man, then ran to catch up with Abuelita before I lost her.

I popped the taffy into my mouth. It was warm and gooey, and so very good. I'd have to buy some to take home as gifts. Jayden would love it.

Abuelita startled me when she spoke. "We have good candy, but I like cake. We no have good cake. Is too dry."

I remembered Adriana's comment about the Twinkies. If Abuelita's weakness was baked goods, I wasn't ashamed to use it to stay on her good side. "I might be able to help you with that."

"You bake?" I could tell from her tone of voice that I had moved up in her estimation.

"I love to bake, but I try to avoid it because of the calories."

Abuelita stopped, looking me up and down. She poked me in the stomach and pinched me in the arm before I could react. "You look like woman. You be proud. How I suffer with Adi…," she clucked her tongue and resumed her march down the sidewalk. "She so skinny!" She threw her bony hands up toward the heavens as if being thin was some horrible sin.

"Bertha!" called a gentle voice from the other side of the street.

Abuelita grabbed my arm, pulling me. "Quick or she see us!"

"Yoo hoo! Bertha!" repeated the voice.

"I think she already did," I said, looking over my shoulder to see a round, elderly woman with short, curly, gray hair poofing around full cheeks and pink horn-rimmed glasses that magnified her eyes. She looked like a cute, little barn owl with poodle hair and I instantly liked her.

Abuelita glared at me. "You too slow. Now she come with us."

The sweet, older lady joined us. I was only five foot five inches, but she barely reached my shoulder. Stuffing the empty plastic bag she held in her pocket and clasping my hand between hers, she said, "My name Rosa. I first sister. You call me Tia Rosa, okay?"

"You old," grumbled Abuelita.

"And more wise," agreed Rosa without losing a beat. "I go with you. You Jessica, yes? You tell me about you, okay?" she patted my hand, and we continued walking as she asked me questions.

The sidewalk opened up to a large park complete with basketball courts and a miniature soccer field. There were trees for shade with benches under them. Kids swirled around on a tire swing, screaming in delight. There was a line for the slide, and a cool-looking zip line that took off from the top of a castle and ended in a dirt pit. It looked like fun. If I was fifty pounds lighter and fifteen years younger, I would have been all over that. I wondered if the park would be empty early the next morning…

Abuelita bumped into me as a pack of dogs burst past us, heading toward the crowded park. "Ay, caramba!" she exclaimed, wobbling to gain her balance and stepping on my sandaled feet with her thick heels. Ignoring the stabbing pain in my foot, I reached out to help her, grabbing her by the shoulders and holding them steady before she fell in the pea gravel surrounding the play area.

"Stupid dogs," she complained.

"It take one for to know one," Tia Rosa mumbled.

The pack of growling dogs circled around and lunged at a trembling puppy in the center of the group. A whimper escaped the poor animal.

Abuelita tugged on my arm. "Come. We leave, they no harm anyone."

But they meant harm to the scrawny dog trapped in the middle of the circle they'd formed. I guessed she was a female from the pink collar hanging loosely around her neck. She was just a puppy, her large feet and floppy ears dwarfing her emaciated body.

A male dog three times her size lunged at her, nipping her on the ear.

I filled my hand with tiny rocks. Hurling them at the dogs, I shouted, "Leave her alone!" Grabbing another handful, I pelted the mangy animals with gravel, scooping up more to have ready. The cowards ran away, leaving the poor, shaking dog alone.

The little pup stood in place, too scared even to move. Dropping my voice, I said, "It's okay now, little lady. You'd best go home now." I waved my hands slowly in front of her to shoo her away without scaring her more than she already was, and my heart broke when she flinched. Wherever her home was, if indeed she still had one, they hadn't been nice to her. They didn't feed her well either. I could count the ribs beneath her fur. Had she not been wearing a collar, I would have assumed she was a stray.

"That stupid," Abuelita said, bursting my humanitarian bubble.

"Why? They were tormenting a defenseless dog. They were acting like bullies, and I couldn't not do something about it."

She shrugged her shoulders, nudging her chin to

something behind me. "You make friend. Now friend follow you and you have to feed it."

Sure enough, the little pup sat in the shade of my shadow, her pink tongue hanging out of her mouth and her large, brown eyes looking up at me in adoration. It was hard not reach down to scratch behind her perky, black and brown ears, but I restrained myself. I was only visiting. It wouldn't be fair to get a pet only to leave her in a month.

"You no heart, Bertha. She sweet puppy!" Tia Rosa reached down and the puppy gently placed a paw in her hand. "And she smart! She shake my hand like young lady."

"Let's go! Maybe she no follow," said Abuelita.

"You don't think she belongs to someone, do you?" I asked, doubting such a skinny dog could have a home — collar or not.

Abuelita harrumphed. "I no like animals. They make mess in kitchen."

Tia Rosa said, "I love animals, but I no have room."

Once we passed the park the neighborhood deteriorated. Paint chipped off the sides of the houses, the yards I could see through the tall fences weren't well-kept, and kids played barefoot in the middle of the street.

Three men hovered around the hood of a yellow cab at a mechanic's shop, sipping beer they poured from a giant, brown Pilsener bottle. I recognized one of them. Bad Tattoo Guy. He frowned when his two buddies whistled at us as we passed, but their harassing calls were drowned out when two police cars with sirens blaring and lights flashing sped past us, their tires screeching as they made a hard left up a narrow alleyway between a store advertising beer and ice cream and a place offering massages.

Abuelita and Tia Rosa looked at each other.

"Maria live up little street." Abuelita pointed at the alley the police cars had disappeared into.

We walked slowly to the end of the alley, the little dog trotting behind us. The lane opened up wide enough for a car to turn around in, and at the end of it were two houses with the police cars parked on either side of a black Audi SUV. I couldn't tell which house the police had gone into. They must have been in a hurry.

I, of course, chose the wrong house — the one that looked like it had people in it.

"No, not that one. That is where Martha, sister of Maria, live."

"Really? Do they have a brother named Lazarus?" I couldn't help myself.

Tia Rosa giggled. "Martha has son name Jesus." She leaned into me and we both laughed.

Abuelita didn't share in our biblical joke. She crossed her arms and tapped her foot.

Trying to be serious, I commented, "It's admirable they live so close to each other. They must be a tight-knit family."

As much as I loved my sisters, I would not like to

be their neighbor. Jessamyn was way more social than I was and didn't understand how I could possibly prefer to spend a night in with a good book and a cup of tea when I could go out and party with her. And Jessenia would drive me nuts with her attempts to impose her demanding housecleaning routine on me. She believed in dusting and vacuuming every single day, while I sometimes went all day without making my bed. The shame!

"Pshaw! They fight always. Is bad live too close with family," said Abuelita.

I looked at her askance, wondering if I dared mention that she lived with her daughter, near her grandkids and, most likely, very near her sister.

She beat me to it. Pointing her finger at me, she said, "I know what you thinking. Children are different. Brothers and sisters," she waved her finger back and forth while clucking her tongue, "they no should live so close."

Tia Rosa puffed out her chest. "If you no like to live next to me, you can move."

"I no move. I bought house first."

Breaking them up before we drew the police's attention, I suggested we ring the buzzer at the gate. Tia Rosa pressed the button and Abuelita shoved her aside to lean into the intercom.

When the door buzzed loudly, I jumped back. A policeman with a machine gun like I'd only seen in the movies opened the gate and shouted at us.

"Let me do talk," Abuelita said, as if I was capable of doing anything other than listen.

Abuelita stretched herself up to all of her five feet in heels and lit into the man with the gun, slapping the barrel away from us as she did.

"Abuelita!" I exclaimed.

"It no dangerous. They no have bullets ... most of time."

Oh great! I was staying in a town where the police carried guns with no bullets? Not that I would feel much better if they did. However, if Abuelita knew his gun wasn't loaded, surely criminals knew it too.

Abuelita seemed to have everything under control, but when she went silent and turned to me, I felt the blood drain from my face.

"What happened?" I asked.

Tia Rosa answered. "Maria dead."

Abuelita nodded her head gravely. "Murder."

Chapter 5

I felt like I'd had the wind knocked out of me. Maria was murdered? Sinking my hands down to my knees, I tried to calm the spinning in my head.

Abuelita jumped away from me. "I polish shoes this morning," she explained. They were shiny.

"I'm not going to throw up. I just don't feel very well and I'm a bit dizzy. It's not every day someone I know is murdered in their own house. I mean, I just saw her an hour and a half ago. I listened to her and José fight most of the way from Ambato to Baños, and it's shocking to know she's gone." I looked up at her through the hair falling over my face, puffing it away to see her better.

A cell phone beeped and the officer guarding the door answered it. When he tucked his phone back in the holder looped around his belt, he widened his stance, thus communicating his resolve not to let us in.

I didn't need to know Spanish to understand his body language.

Using his gun to point to me (which decidedly did not help calm my frazzled nerves and roiling stomach), he said something to Abuelita of which she nodded in approval. Turning back to me, she translated, "He no permit us inside. Is violent crime, and they call Dinased agent."

"Violent? Dinased?" I tried to focus on her words instead of the bile stinging my throat.

"Dinased special..." she wiggled her fingers and looked up to the sky.

"Detective," supplied Tia Rosa. "Dinased special detective division of police. They investigate crimes very violent." She looked down her nose at her sister, an impressive feat considering she was an inch shorter than Abuelita (sans fluffy, gray hair).

Abuelita grumbled. "Now you think you English more good."

"My English *better*," replied Tia Rosa, growing in self-importance (if not in height) at her improved vocabulary.

"Jessica tell us," demanded Abuelita. Crossing her arms and tapping one of her polished heels, she asked, "Who speak *better* English?"

The sisters looked at me to judge. That was a fight I was smart enough to stay out of. As the professional conflict manager in my family, I knew that if I took sides, the senseless bickering would never stop and I would come out the loser.

"Please, I feel sick. Can we sit?"

Abuelita smacked her sister across the arm. "She sick and you fight."

"You fight too!"

"Please, ladies!" I begged, clutching my stomach as I let go of my knees to stand.

Abuelita looped her arm through mine, jabbing me in the ribs with her bony elbow. "She like me more than she like you."

Really? Were we in kindergarten or something?

Tia Rosa took my other arm, gently patting my hand. "We see about that."

Abuelita squinted her eyes at me, and I could see the wheels turning in her head. She looked back at the officer guarding the house and then back at me. Pinching her lips together and rubbing her chin, she was the picture of a woman deep in thought. It was disconcerting.

I wished she would say something. Anything. All I wanted at that moment was to go home and forget all about Baños. Or travel in general really. So far, aside from meeting a few nice people, travel had not been kind to me. In fact, I rather thought it held something against me.

"I have idea. Come," Abuelita said, already on the move and walking toward the metal door next to Maria's house. With a loud knock, she shouted, "Martha!"

Tia Rosa explained in case I hadn't remembered, "Martha is Maria's sister."

Abuelita added, "The police tell nothing. I ask Martha."

A teenage girl with black and blue striped hair opened the rusty door.

"My mom is in the kitchen," the girl said in a monotone, turning her back and leading us into the house.

Oh good, someone else who spoke English. Not that I didn't trust Abuelita or Tia Rosa to translate well enough, but I had a growing suspicion that they left out what they didn't consider important enough to repeat. The officer hadn't needed to point his gun at me only to inform us that a special detective was working the case.

The girl took a seat in a living room full of people. She rolled her heavily Kohl-lined eyes at them before plunking down on the plastic covered couch.

Abuelita said, "You stay with Fernanda. Rosa come with me."

When Tia Rosa didn't follow her immediately, Abuelita added between pinched lips, "We give condolence to Martha and use bathroom." Her eyes darted toward the back of the house.

My fear that there was more going on than met the eye was confirmed when Tia Rosa lit up like a light bulb in understanding of her sister's hidden agenda. "Ah! Yes, the bathroom. I drink tea and need bathroom. Bertha drink coffee and need bathroom. We go to bathroom."

Abuelita grimaced. I did too. It was a bit overkill. "They know where we go! Less talk, more walk."

They bickered all the way to the back of the living room and disappeared through the first open doorway.

Not knowing what else to do, I sat down next to Martha's daughter on the plastic-covered furniture. It squeaked and made all sorts of rude noises as I tried to get comfortable on the extra firm cushions. Seriously, I may as well have sat on the hardwood floor for all the coziness the couch offered. The plastic was the cherry on top.

Feeling awkward and very much like an outsider, I asked the teen, "What's your name?"

"Fernanda." Without making any attempt at eye contact, she pulled out her smart phone and tapped her black fingernails against the screen.

I tried not to stare at the crowd of assembled people, at second glance mostly kids younger than Fernanda, scattered on the other side of the room facing the TV on the back wall. Someone sitting in a chair with toddlers crawling along the cushions played a violent video game. Definitely not something I'd allow my nephew, Jayden, to watch. I cringed and looked away when blood splattered against the plasma screen. Ew. Kind of inappropriate under the circumstances...

A few adults milled about the room, talking and drinking from plastic cups.

I identified the owner of the fancy SUV parked

outside. He was as out of place in the room as his car was outside. He wore white golf shorts and a Hawaiian shirt unbuttoned low enough to show off his chest hair. He held a Panama hat with a leather headband in his hands. Both of his little fingers had thick, gold rings with a sparkling jewel in the middle. His black hair was slicked back Grease-style.

Fernanda heaved a bored sigh, pulling my attention away from the other people in the room. Why wasn't she crying? Why was nobody crying?

I gave her a few minutes to say something, but when she showed no signs of engaging in any sort of conversation, my curiosity eventually won out. "Your English is very good. Where did you learn?"

With a huff, she looked up from her cell phone. "They teach English at school here. In case you haven't noticed, Baños is full of tourists and it's in our best interest to speak fluently."

Smart Alec. Fine. I guess the direct approach was the way to go with her.

"I had noticed. I understand you were not very close to Maria. She was your aunt, right?"

She set her phone down. That was progress.

Leaning forward and adopting a rebellious tone, Fernanda said, "She was my aunt. But nobody in this room can be truly sad that she's dead." She leaned back against the squeaky couch, crossing her arms and lifting her chin. She clearly expected a reaction from me.

I had noticed a definite volatility in Maria (at least,

toward her husband when he corrected her English), but it was sad to hear how nobody — not even her family — liked her.

"I didn't know Maria very well. She drove me from the Quito airport to here and I left my backpack in her trunk by mistake. I went to her house hoping I'd be able to get it."

"Good luck with that. She was murdered in her car. If your bag was still there, the police would have it now."

My stomach started churning again. I didn't know the details of the crime, but I couldn't help but hope that there hadn't been any blood involved. I'm optimistic like that.

Apparently sensing my wooziness and seeking to capitalize on it, Fernanda leaned forward and whispered, "It was done with a machete." She ran her finger across her neck. "At least, that's what they suspect because of the depth of the cut."

Okay, so there was blood. Probably lots of blood.

Desperately needing to change the subject before I tossed my cookies, and deeply disturbed at her attitude toward her aunt's murder, I asked, "Who are these people?"

"You see the man playing the game? That's my uncle José, Maria's husband. You would have met him already if Maria drove you home from Quito. He just got home from Miami." Her words were curt, but her face softened as she looked at him.

An elderly woman walked across the room and

gave José a hug, patting his back and speaking in a low tone. He shrugged her off and held up his control.

"Is that his mother and children?"

"No, that's just the neighbor lady. Half of the people here are just neighbors waiting around to hear what they can so they can gossip about it later. Stuff like this doesn't happen in Baños. The kids crawling around Uncle José are my little brothers and sisters."

I counted five children. Every one of them was younger than Fernanda. "All of them?"

"I'm the oldest. There are too many of us. At least, that's what my dad thought when he left us a year ago ... right after the last baby was born."

A little girl, maybe four years old, skipped over to us. Her bangs spiked up and her hair fell in chunks around her face. Red lipstick stained her lips and cheeks.

Fernanda smirked at her. "This is Ana Paola. She tried to cut her own hair yesterday, and she got into my mom's makeup this morning."

Ana Paola beamed up at me, leaning her little hands with bright yellow fingernails against my knees.

"Lovely. You're a makeup artist in the making," I told her, smiling and reaching out to smooth her spikes.

"She's a pest," Fernanda said in a monotone. "She steals my eyeliner all the time and she's currently obsessed with my neon nail polishes. She drew smiley faces with it all over the house. Even on Mom's machete. Wouldn't it be ironic if that was the machete used to kill my Aunt Maria?"

Was this girl serious? She sounded happy her aunt was gone.

Tia Rosa came out with a loaded tray. It had an assortment of cookies and candy on it. When she had offered it to every person in the room, she set it on a small table near the tearless mourners.

Another woman came out of the kitchen with another tray full of plastic cups with steaming, yellow liquid in them. Her red-rimmed eyes darted around the room until they settled on Fernanda.

"Take one," said Tia Rosa, grabbing the plastic cup with her fingertips along the upper rim. "Is chamomile tea. Good for stomach."

The boiling beverage burned my fingers as I took it from her, careful not to squish the cup and spill hot tea everywhere until I could situate my fingers around the rim as Tia Rosa had done.

The woman with the tray of tea stood with us. She looked more exhausted up close and, unlike everyone else in the room, there was evidence of tears on her streaked cheeks. Her resemblance to Maria was striking, only she looked softer … nicer.

I didn't know what to say. Really, who does when someone dies suddenly and unexpectedly? 'I'm sorry for your loss,' just didn't seem to cut it … and even worse in a foreign language. But even if she didn't understand me, I still had to say something.

"I'm so sorry," I said.

Her chin quivered, as did her hands holding the tray with two more cups looking like they were about to melt on it. Tia Rosa took it from her before she burned herself.

Fernanda put her arm around her mom and rested her head against her shoulder. Martha kissed her on the forehead. Her eyebrows furrowed together in worry as she gazed at her daughter.

"Thank you," said Martha in a thick accent. "I love Maria. Maria good sister." She wiped her eyes.

Fernanda removed her arm and stepped away from her mom, her expression full of disgust. Taking the tray away from Tia Rosa, she took it to the kitchen.

Martha called after her, but Fernanda ignored her. Looking around nervously, Martha wrung her hands together. "Teenager," she said, trying to explain her daughter's behavior with a word. As if her age explained everything. When Fernanda returned, she had her cell phone firmly planted in front of her face.

Tia Rosa used one of the few Spanish words I knew all too well. Baño. I wondered if that's where Abuelita had disappeared to and what the great attraction was to Martha's bathroom.

"I'll be back," Tia Rosa said before departing from the room again.

"Okay, Arnold," I mumbled, which elicited a snort from Fernanda.

Martha sat on the arm of a chair next to José. The baby wobbled over to her. She scooped her up in her arms, kissing her cheeks and smoothing her brown curls. It struck me that Martha was the sort of woman who would not cry in front of her children. They leaned on her for support as they watched the gory game. I almost started crying for her when I wondered how I would feel if Jessamyn or Jessenia were forever gone to me and I had the burden of grieving while life carried on and there were mouths to feed. I remembered how hard it had been for my dad. How hard it still was.

Growing up, I had begged my mom and dad to put Jessenia or Jessamyn (or both!) up for adoption — as most siblings are guilty of doing. As we had grown, we couldn't wait to move away from each other. However, after a week or so of what we thought would be glorious freedom, we found ways to keep in touch every day thereafter. Texts, messages, calls… Rarely did a day go by when we didn't communicate with each other. We got on each other's nerves and we were as different as night is from day, but they were my sisters. And I loved them every bit as much as I knew they loved me. We took care of each other.

I doubted Fernanda gave her mom much support. I could see the concern in Martha's frequent, worried glances at her oldest girl.

Fernanda looked up from her phone. "Abuelita has been gone a long time and Tia Rosa is acting weird. If they blow up our bathroom, they get to build a new one."

That she believed them capable of doing so

concerned me greatly, much more than my shock at hearing that someone would build a house without an indoor bathroom. "Maybe Abuelita fell in."

I almost laughed at the image running through my mind, but I stopped myself. The last thing I wanted to do was give the impression of being insensitive when the occasion called for quiet melancholy.

Fernanda was not as inhibited as me. Her shoulders shook and a cackle escaped her. "Oh my God, that would be too funny. And for it to happen to Abuelita of all people...." She smiled, revealing a sense of humor behind her sarcastic exterior.

Something she had said earlier bothered me, and I aimed to take advantage of her improved attitude to ask. "Why didn't people like Maria? She seemed a bit rough around the edges, but only your mom has shed a tear for her. Not even José looks bothered."

Fernanda's eyes darted around the room. Leaning closer to me, her voice dropped to a whisper. "Let me just say that I wasn't surprised when she was found murdered in her car. She was not a nice woman. If you ask me, Uncle José is better off without her and now he can marry my mom like I've begged him to do since, like, forever."

Wishful thinking on her part, I thought, watching as José waved the remote around in front of him to shoot at aliens. Would the slip of a girl take matters into her own hands and off her aunt to make her dream come true? Was that why Martha looked so worried? Did she suspect that her own daughter was capable of murder? Who else stood to benefit from killing Maria?

Disturbed by her words and the accusations forming in my head, I asked vaguely, "She had a run-in with a taxi driver and a guy wearing an undershirt and gold chain when we got here. The taxi had dents all over it and the fender had duct tape on it."

"That would be Martin. He's a taxi driver."

"We saw him at the mechanic a block away," I added.

"That's not surprising. He lives nearby. Sometimes he gives me and my brother a ride to school and he never charges — even though he could use the money. He's decent like that."

Not exactly the image of a cold-blooded murderer. "And the other guy? Undershirt and gold chain…."

She sighed and the hint of a smile tempered her harsh makeup. "That's Christian. He went to school with Martin."

"What does he have against your aunt?"

Fernanda twirled a skull ring around her finger. Her eyes darted all over the room. "Nothing as far as I know. He's a sweet guy. More lover than fighter, if you know what I mean."

There was something she wasn't telling me.

Focusing on the solution to the problem rather than on the problem itself soothed my nerves and calmed my stomach. My hands no longer shook. I was no detective, but it gave me something to talk about with Fernanda. I looked around the room and sipped on my cooling tea, wondering who knew more than they would admit to.

Fernanda seemed to read my mind. She said, "The neighbors hated her, but I think it's more likely she was involved in something she shouldn't have been in." She spoke openly. Not like someone who had a secret to hide ... unlike Mr. Fancy Pants, who twirled his diamond ring around his finger and shuffled his Panama hat from side to side in his hands.

"Like what?"

Fernanda lowered her voice. "I don't know what she was into, but she works as a taxi driver and my uncle makes puro for a living. They make decent money, but not enough to justify a new car, the huge TV in their living room, the new gaming system and TV he installed over here, and all the other things they buy. The money has to come from somewhere, doesn't it?"

"What is puro?"

A deep voice behind me answered, "I believe you guys call it moonshine. José makes it from the sugar cane he grows out in his parents' fields and he sells it at a little stand at the bus terminal here. It's powerful stuff, but too rustic to sell at a decent bar such as mine." The Grease extra held his hand out to me. "I'm Dario Vega, owner of The Lava Lounge. I'm the one who found Maria and called the police. Were you a friend of hers?"

"Not exactly. I only met her today. I don't know

anybody here." I could see the confusion on his face. If I only just met her, what was I doing here? I added, "I left my backpack in her car and came with some friends to get it back."

"Friends?" he asked.

Abuelita rushed into the room, answering Dario's question before I could explain how loosely I had used the term. Her face was flushed, her shoes were no longer shiny, and a twig stuck out of her hair. Tia Rosa was right behind her, rubbing her leg and limping.

Chapter 6

Deciding it was safest to keep on Fernanda's good side, I said, "I think we were right. She definitely fell into something."

Fernanda giggled.

Unperturbed, Abuelita hugged Fernanda. "We go now. I send lunch tomorrow."

Fernanda leaned forward and kissed me on the cheek. "It was nice to meet you, Jessica. I had best help my mom. This is really hard on her."

I didn't flinch, so I guessed I was making progress. I even remembered to make a smoochy noise before she pulled away.

Dario smelled like hair pomade and whiskey. He apologized for not being able to give us a ride home, but he had to wait for the detective to arrive. I couldn't help but wonder what business he had with Maria. Did it have something to do with the liquor José had brought back from Miami?

Saying our farewells to everyone else, (rather, I stood and waved awkwardly by the door while Abuelita and Tia Rosa gave their condolences to the rest of the family and neighbors still in the room) my eyes squinted as they got used to the early evening sunshine outside. José didn't even bother to pause his game. I didn't think he even knew I had chatted with his niece for a good twenty minutes while he was engrossed in his entertainment.

Abuelita walked with renewed vigor as we wound our way through the police cars and down the narrow alleyway leading to the paved street and to dinner. Not that I would be able to eat much.

"Why were you gone so long?" I asked, plucking the branch out of Abuelita's ebony hair.

She looked at me sheepishly. "I try find backpack. I climb over concrete wall. Rosa push me."

Tia Rosa smiled up at me, her magnified eyes the image of innocence. "I push her. She pull me."

"You broke into a crime scene to look for my stuff?" I wasn't sure whether I wanted to hug them or shake them by the shoulders for taking such a risk. "What if you had been caught? Didn't it bother you to see ... Maria?" I shivered.

Abuelita waved her hand dismissively. "Is no problem. Newspaper show worse on front page. And I no touch nothing. But I no see bag before she trip over giant feet and police hear. We run before they see us." Abuelita glared at Tia Rosa.

"I sorry, Jessica," Tia Rosa frowned, staring down

at her feet. They were probably two sizes smaller than mine.

Acting on the impulse of the moment, I wrapped my arms around Tia Rosa and Abuelita.

It was like hugging a stiff board and a feather pillow, but I appreciated what they had tried to do for me. I was just really glad they didn't get caught or do anything to incriminate themselves.

As we crossed the street from the alley, I noticed that the little dog was curled up in a shady spot against the wall. As we walked by, she got to her feet and fell in behind us, her ears bouncing and her pink tongue hanging out. She had been waiting for us.

Twisting her lips into a disapproving frown, Abuelita said, "You see? She follow us."

My heart went out to the poor puppy nobody seemed to want. "Let her follow. I'll take her picture and make a poster. Maybe her owners will claim her." It was a stupid thing to say, and I knew it. Even if her owners did claim her, I wouldn't want to give her to them so they could continue to mistreat her.

Abuelita stopped walking. Turning to face me, she poked me in the arm with her pointy finger. "No dog in my kitchen. You understand?"

"Of course not. I can't keep her anyway. I'm only here for a month, but maybe I can find a home for her in that time."

Abuelita glared at me. "You give dog name. Why give name if no keep her?"

What? No I hadn't.

"Is good name. She a little Lady," said Tia Rosa.

Oh, that name. I couldn't argue with her, although I had only said it to calm the pup down after her scare with the big dogs.

Looking at the dog, I asked, "Is that your name? Can we call you Lady?"

The puppy twirled in a circle and barked happily. Lady it was.

Abuelita folded her arms. "You feed her."

"Can we swing by the grocery store I saw on our way here? I'll buy some dog food there."

Tia Rosa clucked her tongue. "She so skinny. Lady need rich food."

Abuelita flew her hands up in the air and strode off without us. "She problem now. You feed her."

ABUELITA AND TIA ROSA showed me into the garden behind the restaurant through a secured gate, Lady happily in tow. She pranced in like she already knew the place.

She looked up the stairs leading to Adriana's apartment, sniffing the air and listening for something. Then, she went up the steps, spun two circles, and laid down in front of the door.

"It rain, she get wet and she stink," grumbled Abuelita.

Tia Rosa agreed. "Better for her under wash tank. Is dry. I ask Adi for pillow."

Lady was happy in her spot, so I didn't call her. She couldn't go in the kitchen anyway.

Jake walked through the swinging door from the dining room, his arms laden with dirty dishes which he took over to the sink and began washing. Watching him help his mom and sister in the kitchen made my heart go pitter patter. And he had brought the phone charger. It lay next to the coffee maker.

"How good of you to show up for the dinner rush," commented Sylvia, looking pointedly at her mom and aunt. "Jake had to fill in for you when one of the other girls came in late. What took so long?"

Tia Rosa and Abuelita raced over to Jake, who squatted down to half his height for them to kiss him on each cheek. Abuelita tried to elbow Tia Rosa out of the way to get to Adriana first, but Tia Rosa was agile (or, more likely, she was used to her sister's tricks) and evaded Abuelita's pointy jabs without losing a step. All signs of her limp were gone. They nearly bowled Adriana over, but she held her ground as they showed their appreciation to her. Abuelita wasn't as gruff as she let on. And Tia Rosa wasn't as clueless as she seemed.

"The orders out?" asked Abuelita, spooning a piece of chicken into a bowl and burning her fingers to separate the meat from the bones.

"Adi just took the last order out and Jake finished cleaning the tables. Why?" Sylvia looked like she wanted to ask her mom what *she* had been doing, but restrained herself for fear of hearing the answer.

When Abuelita took the bowl outside and I heard her heels on the wood steps, I smiled. She was feeding Lady. For all her crustiness, she had a warm heart.

"You never guess what happen," said Abuelita excitedly, the screen door slamming behind her.

"First things first. Are you hungry?" Sylvia pulled out plates and piled them with fluffy, white rice, steamed vegetables, and a piece of chicken with a red sauce that smelled like Heaven. Sprinkling chopped cilantro over the top, she placed a plate in front of me. "This is called seco de pollo. It's chicken in a sauce made of tomatoes, onion, garlic, cumin, beer, and a few local spices. I hope you like it."

I took a bite, and a moan escaped me before I could stop myself.

Abuelita said proudly, "Is my recipe."

"It's delicious!" There was nothing insipid about this chicken, and I attacked my plate with gusto. I hadn't eaten a proper meal in over forty-eight hours, and I hadn't realized until my first bite how hungry I was.

Tia Rosa put six mugs on the table and poured coffee into them. I reached for my cup gladly. It had been a long day. The longest day of my life.

Jake and Adriana did another pass through the dining room. When they joined us, Sylvia asked, "Okay, spill it. What happened at Maria's?"

"She murdered," said Tia Rosa before Abuelita could open her mouth.

Cabs, Cakes, and Corpses

Abuelita, not one to be bested, added, "She murdered in car with machete."

Sylvia, Jake, and Adriana unanimously set their coffee mugs down. "What?!"

Tia Rosa started her narration from the time she left her art class, including our encounter with Lady. From there, Abuelita took over, telling about her friendly chat with the policeman and our visit to Martha. She conveniently left out the small detail of her and Tia Rosa's break-in to Maria's garage. I didn't want to get them in trouble, so I didn't mention it either.

Jake furrowed his eyebrows. "Why would someone kill Maria?"

"She mean. People no like her," said Abuelita.

"You mean. People no kill you," said Tia Rosa.

"That's not reason enough to kill someone. People haven't liked her for years. Why now? Why her?" he insisted.

I could help here. "Fernanda told me she thinks her aunt was into something dangerous. She couldn't justify how José and Maria were able to buy a new car and all the electronics they have."

"I guess I'd never thought about it," said Adriana. "I just assumed they'd saved."

Jake explained, "Cars are expensive here because of import taxes. Maria's new car probably cost them around thirty thousand dollars. With minimum wage being just over three hundred dollars a month, it would take forever to save that amount. Even with both of them working."

I almost choked on my coffee. "Three hundred dollars a month? How do people live on that?" Even with the lower cost of living here, it would be nearly impossible to manage on so little. No wonder Martha looked so tired. She probably had to work several jobs just to keep her five kids fed and clothed.

"Is hard," acknowledged Abuelita. "Ah, before I no remember, I want give food for Martha. She need help."

"I'd be glad to send lunches for the next few days. She works so hard and has all those kids." Sylvia wiped her hand across her forehead. "Without Maria's help, she's going to have a harder time."

Adriana asked in a soft voice, "You don't think she could have done it, do you? Maybe out of jealousy or something?"

"I no give food to killer!" said Abuelita angrily. "She no have reason to kill sister. I think José kill wife."

That's where I'd put my money too. Or maybe it was the bar owner. "He didn't act like a man who had just lost his wife. However, Fernanda didn't say as much, but I think she suspects Dario Vega. There's something strange going on there."

"Why was he there?" asked Adriana.

"He found Maria's body and called the police."

"Where was José?" she asked.

"I don't know, and he was too busy playing video

games for me to ask. He acted like nothing had happened."

"Could it be he was in shock?" suggested Jake.

"More like he didn't care, but I don't know him well enough to say. What I do know is that I was more affected by her murder than he seemed to be — and she was practically a stranger to me. That's just not normal."

"Shouldn't he have been talking to the police?" Adriana asked.

"They wait special detective," answered Abuelita.

"Maybe that's why he was acting strangely. The police wouldn't want him talking to people until the agent got there for his statement," suggested Jake.

Sylvia tapped her fingers against her lips, pausing to say, "When I called over there earlier this afternoon, Maria answered the phone. I heard two men fighting in the background. That must have been right before she was killed."

"You know who was it?" Abuelita asked.

"I assumed one of the men was José, but I couldn't hear well enough to identify anyone with certainty. Nor did I hear what they fought about. Maria got off the phone too quickly. Just to think that may have been her last phone call…" Sylvia's words trailed off.

"Maybe it Dario," suggested Tia Rosa.

We hovered around the island in silence. It was like a scene from an Agatha Christie mystery where all the friends and family of the murder victim get involved to bring the killer to justice with the help of an observant sleuth. Except I was no Miss Marple. Just the thought of blood made me queasy. No, I was here on vacation and I aimed to hit every souvenir shop in the morning, lay in a hammock like tourists are supposed to do in tropical climates, and finish off the day at the pub Jake and Adriana had told me about. I would be a proper vacationer and leave the investigation to the professionals.

Picking up the empty plates, I thanked Sylvia for the yummy food and washed the dishes. I'd had more than enough excitement for one day. I needed to take a picture of Lady, plug my phone in to charge, and fall into bed as soon as I'd talked to my family.

Tia Rosa bumped me away from the sink with her hip. "You tired. I wash."

Thanking her, I dried my hands before picking up the charger. "Thank you for remembering this. As soon as I get my stuff from Maria's trunk, I'll return it."

"Keep it as long as you need it." Jake had a dimple in his right cheek. Had he no flaws?

"I'm going to take a pic of Lady and see if my family can make their call earlier," I announced to let anyone who cared know my plans.

Sylvia pulled me into an embrace. "You've had an eventful day, haven't you? Rest well, Jess. Let us know if you need anything, okay?"

She released her hold and Abuelita startled me by

stepping between us. Seriously, personal space was a foreign concept in Ecuador.

"You tell family about murder?" she asked.

My answer was immediate. "Absolutely not." Why give them reason to worry when they were thousands of miles away and could do nothing but regret their unanimous decision to send me away on an adventure? I bet they didn't have this in mind!

Adriana exhaled deeply. "Oh, good. We were so worried you'd be on the first flight back to Oregon."

Abuelita reached up and patted my cheek. "Is good you stay."

I didn't feel awkward, even though everyone in the room looked at me. They really seemed to want me there. Even Abuelita. A strange sense of comfort wrapped its arms around me just as they so often did. I had only met the Jimenez family that afternoon, but they had already managed to make me feel like I belonged with them. That they wanted me, not for what I could do for them, but just for me was really nice.

"Tomorrow, you bake me sugar treat?" asked Abuelita.

Okay, well maybe they weren't entirely altruistic.

Chapter 7

I woke the next morning to sunshine warming my face through the window overlooking the side street. I'd been so tired and it'd been so dark the night before, I'd forgotten to close the curtains. Roosters crowed and dogs barked. Unlatching the window, I pushed it open to let the daylight wake me up. Inhaling the fresh morning air, the comforting smell of baking bread filled my lungs. My stomach grumbled. I must have slept late. Not unusual for me. I never had been an early riser.

Padding barefoot out to the kitchen, I saw Adriana sketching in a notebook, a look of intense concentration on her face.

"Good morning," I said softly, wanting to be polite without interrupting what she had going on.

"Wow, you're up early. I thought for sure you'd sleep in." She pointed to the coffee maker. "Want some?"

Early? I looked outside. It was most definitely daytime, and from the looks of things, had been for some time.

She laughed. "You're completely turned around, aren't you? It's six thirty right now. That would be, what, four thirty in Portland?"

"Six thirty? I never wake up before eight, and even then it's only after slapping the snooze button at least four times." I was the only night owl in a family of morning larks. They'd get a kick out of hearing that I'd gotten out of bed so early my first morning of vacation in Baños.

Adriana ran her finger down a list of scribbled notes by her sketch.

"What are you doing up so early?" I asked.

"I'm perfecting my drawing before I start cutting into fabric. My dream is to design retro-inspired clothes for women of all shapes and sizes, but there's more money in bridal and pageant gowns. I'm determined to dress one of the Reinas in next year's Festival."

"Reinas?"

"It means 'Queen.' It's what they call the beauty contestants during Carnival. It's a big deal down here and it would mean lots of exposure and publicity for me."

"Impressive. What is this sketch for?" It was something I'd wear. An A-line, tea-length gown with a fitted, straight neckline. Very classy.

"Some design ideas for bridesmaid's gowns. A

friend of mine is getting married soon and she asked me to give her a hand. There'll be sequins littered all over my clean floor next week. It's a small price to pay for my dream."

Her dream. I wasn't brave enough to go for my dream. I'd checked into it and the list of licenses and permits needed to open a simple bakery was enough to send me to the community college for web classes. It wasn't my dream, but it paid a decent wage.

Adriana closed her notebook. "Anyway, that's enough about me. I saw you eyeing my KitchenAid…."

"I promised Abuelita I'd make her cake. My grandma sent some of her favorite recipes with me, and I thought I'd give one a try. She specializes in baked and fried goods. Given the extra humidity and heat here, I think I'd better start with something simple." The perfect recipe came to mind. Goofballs! Bite-sized doughnut holes, fried and dipped in chocolate frosting.

"Sounds fantastic! Poor Abuelita suffers so much. She's the only one in our family with an insatiable sweet tooth. The rest of us prefer salty treats. I could eat a family-size bag of Doritos all by myself."

"All this talk of food is making me hungry." My stomach growled loud enough for her to hear.

"We'd better do something about that then. Mom will be in the kitchen with fresh-baked rolls from the bakery."

Changing my clothes and tossing my hair up into

a ponytail in record time, I opened the front door to a tail-wagging puppy. She danced on her hind legs when she saw us.

"What a lady! She's too polite to jump all over us like most dogs. Doesn't she have the cutest little brown face and the biggest, darkest puppy eyes? She even wears eye liner," said Adriana, dropping down on her knees to scratch Lady behind the ears. The happy puppy flipped onto her back. Like her face, her stomach was brown while the rest of her body was black. Her pink collar caught between the planks of wood and Adriana had to pull it loose.

"That reminds me … is there a place I can print off a bunch of pictures so I can post them around town?"

"There's a print shop across the street, but they won't open for another couple hours."

Abuelita met us as we were going down the stairs. She had a bowl of water in one hand and a bowl of what looked like porridge with chunks of meat, bones, and cartilage floating in it. Not so appetizing for anyone but a furry friend Abuelita insisted was a pest.

Lady came down the stairs behind us and I witnessed Abuelita pat her on the head when the puppy looked up at her thankfully before licking daintily at a bone sticking out of the bowl.

Adriana leaned in to whisper. "I almost hope nobody claims her. She didn't make a mess of the garden and she didn't bark all night. She's not much of a guard dog, but it might be nice to have a pet back here. Even Abuelita has taken a liking to her."

It would be the perfect solution. Lady would have a good home here. I noticed the fluffed pillow set out for her under the wash tank as we walked past. She must have spent all night on the stairs, preferring to be close to Adriana and me than to food.

The kitchen smelled heavenly. Like coffee and bread.

Abuelita, Tia Rosa, Sylvia, and Jake sat around the island, a giant bowl of bread surrounded by strawberry jam, white cheese, and hardboiled eggs.

Sylvia held up a pitcher. "Pineapple juice?" she asked.

"Yum!" I replied.

"How was your call last night?" she asked, filling everyone's glasses.

"It was nice to see my family. They were happy to know I finally made it here okay."

"Why did you get here a day late?" asked Jake.

After a night's rest, my trials of the two days before didn't seem so horrible. Especially after what had happened to Maria. So, I gave them a humorous retelling of most of the events of the previous days. It struck me as funny how my backpack, which I had defended tooth and nail at the airport, had been left carelessly in the trunk. They were appropriately impressed with Jessenia's forethought in writing lists of packed items and how it had helped me get my stuff back. I sighed at the loss of my e-reader.

"You like to read?" asked Jake.

I sighed again. Like wasn't a strong enough word. Powell's book store had been my second home. It was the reason I'd rented an apartment in the Pearl District when rent was cheaper elsewhere. "I love to read."

"Really? What's your favorite genre?" he asked.

"Do I have to choose? It depends on my mood, I guess. I like memoirs and self-help books in the morning. They help me start my day off in a better mood. For public transportation, I read the highly acclaimed literature so I can look smart while getting lost in beautiful prose. For the park, I prefer romcoms. The lightheartedness suits the atmosphere. It's a little contradictory, but I like to read mysteries and thrillers at night so I can spend the next hour too scared to sleep. I take my reader with me everywhere in case I have to wait. It's old and has a crack in the bottom right corner of the screen, but I can't replace it because it's my friend." Maybe it sounded a little pathetic, but it brought me happiness.

"That's cool," he said. "You should go to Casa Hood. They have a library of English books they're constantly trading with travelers passing through and looking to swap novels."

"That is the best news I've had all day! I was planning on looking around the shops this morning. I want to buy gifts for my family, and figured now is as good a time as any. Is Casa Hood close?"

"I'll give you directions."

Awesome! My day was off to a promising start.

THREE HOURS LATER, I returned to Adi's apartment with three books from Casa Hood's library, a bag of dog food small enough for me to lug home, and an assortment of souvenirs. I'd found the coolest outdoor market tucked between busy streets where they sold handwoven scarves in bold colors, hammocks, jewelry made out of tagua nuts, and painted figurines carved from balsa wood. I also bought pulled taffy in assorted fruit flavors. Jessenia would hate how sticky it would make Jayden, but he would love it. I dumped my treasures on my bed and went downstairs to see about giving Lady a bath.

I went into the kitchen to ask Sylvia if she had a wash basin I could use for Lady. A man with a buzz cut and the kind of thick build only one who knew how to use weights could have stood with his booted feet hip-width apart. He wore a black polo shirt with a pocket. In his hands, he held a notepad and pen. A scar from his ear to the corner of his mouth told me he was not a stranger to violence.

"Miss James?" he asked in almost perfect English.

"Yes," I answered, feeling silly when I realized that I stood at attention.

He held out his hand for a handshake, which I took with a nervous glance at Sylvia. "I am Agent Washington Vasquez from special investigations. I understand you were one of the last people to see Maria alive. I have some questions for you."

Sylvia smiled reassuringly at me. "Might I suggest you use one of the tables in our dining area? I'll make some more juice and bring it out to you in a moment."

"Thank you, Mrs. Jimenez."

"Please, Agent Vasquez, call me Sylvia. Mrs. Jimenez is my mother or my aunt."

"Both of them are Jimenez?" I asked, puzzled.

"They married brothers," she explained quickly. Agent Vasquez was not the kind of guy one kept waiting.

He nodded curtly and we went out to the dining room. Adi sat behind the register and, when Agent Vasquez stopped in front of her, clearly wishing she'd get up and leave so he could intimidate me in peace, she smiled and waved. "Is there anything I can get you, Agent Vasquez?"

He turned with a grunt, and I mouthed, "Thank you," to Adi. With a wink, she rested her arms against the counter and settled in. She wasn't going anywhere.

The questions began before my bum hit the hot pink and gold upholstered cushion of the pine chair. "Miss James, I understand you spent a few hours with Maria Guzmán yesterday. What was your business with her?"

"She drove me and her husband, José, from the Quito airport."

"What time was it when you arrived here?" he asked, pencil poised over the paper of his notepad.

"It was around four in the afternoon."

"One of my officers said you later went to Señora Guzmán's home. Why?"

"Oh, the guy with the machine gun. Is that necessary?" I asked, genuinely stumped as to why he needed to pack such heavy artillery in the small, peaceful town.

Agent Vasquez didn't answer my question. "Why did you go to Señora Guzmán's home?"

"She left before I could get my backpack out of the trunk. Maybe you saw it? It's green and—"

"There was no backpack in the trunk or anywhere else in the car when we searched the vehicle."

"But, I left it there. Maybe it got mixed in with their stuff when they unloaded the car and it's inside their house? Are you sure it wasn't in the trunk?"

He cast me a long-suffering glance. "The trunk was completely empty. Now, if you will allow me to ask the questions, I have a murder case to solve."

Feeling like a scolded child, I shoved my hands under my thighs and waited for him to speak.

"Did Señora Guzmán take any calls during the trip or speak to anyone besides you or Señor Guzmán?"

"She hardly spoke to me at all. She was too busy fighting with her husband." I wondered if José was the main suspect. "Oh, and when we got here, she got into a yelling match with another taxi driver — a guy named Martin and his friend, Christian."

He nodded his head. "That's consistent with what Señor Guzmán told me. Is there anything else you remember? Any impressions or details which struck you as out of place during your drive from Quito to here?"

Only one memory surfaced. "It probably means nothing, but when José came out of the airport, he had some bottles of liquor with him."

Agent Vasquez looked up abruptly. "Bottles? How many?"

"Three. One whiskey, one vodka, and one aguardiente."

He scribbled in his notepad. "Interesting. Anything else?"

"Well, it just struck me as unusual that Maria seemed much more excited to see the liquor than she did her husband. You don't think that could have anything to do with her murder, do you? Would someone kill for something so common?"

"You would be surprised, Miss James. Right now, I have to follow every lead and possibility. The information you shared may provide us with a motive and lead us to our killer. Is there anything else you remember? Anything else that seemed unusual?"

Like Fernanda's gruesome comments about her aunt's murder? I wasn't about to sic a detective on the girl. If he was any good at his job, and I suspected he was, he'd figure that out right away without me pointing it out to him. And then, there was Dario Vega. He was a smooth customer. "It seemed odd to me that Dario Vega was the one to find Maria. Why was he there?"

"Allow me to reassure you that Señor Vega's alibi checks out. I hope this experience won't affect your visit more than it needs to. It would be a pity." He reached into his pocket and pulled out a card. "This is my phone number. If you remember anything at all, please give me a call. Everything is important and no detail is too small for my consideration." He looked at me so intently, I felt I had to answer.

"I'll call you if I remember anything."

"Okay, I'll let you go for now. You're staying here?"

"Yes."

"Don't venture too far. You were one of the last people to see her alive, and you may have seen and understood more than you give yourself credit for."

Sylvia came out with the glasses of juice she had promised. Agent Vasquez downed his in a couple giant gulps, thanked us, and left.

As soon as he was out of sight, Abuelita and Tia Rosa came into the dining room. Their eyes darted around.

"He leave?" asked Abuelita.

Sylvia sighed. "You're safe now, Mom. You too, Tia. I doubt he came here to arrest you for whatever it was you did back in the seventies."

I chuckled, teasing them, "You've been on the wrong side of the law? Why is that not surprising?"

Cabs, Cakes, and Corpses

The sisters looked at each other, but said nothing.

"You don't know the half of it. Now, I'm going back to the kitchen," Sylvia said, sweeping the empty glasses from the table and taking Adi with her through the swinging doors. Tia Rosa followed, turning every so often to stare with her owlish eyes at Abuelita and jerk her head in my direction. It made me nervous.

"You not lose money in backpack?" Abuelita asked in a low tone as soon as they were gone.

What were they up to? "No..." I answered cautiously. "Why?"

"We split cost. You pay ten dollar. I pay ten dollar. Rosa pay ten dollar."

"Dare I ask what for?"

She blinked like I was an idiot.

"Fine. My money belt has taken a hit today anyway. What's ten dollars more?"

Abuelita blew a raspberry. "I see tourist wear money belt outside the pants. I ask you: What does that do? Tell thief, "Here my money! I have so much money, I put it in special cloth belt you cut with knife and steal? Is estúpido."

"Tell me how you really feel," I mumbled.

"Is how I feel. Is estúpido," she answered. I would have to be careful with her. She understood way more English than she let on. I bet she even knew how to use verbs properly, but chose not to do it to put people like me at a disadvantage.

She looked up and smiled at me, and I just knew she could read my mind.

Deciding that openness was the best option with someone as unpredictable as her, I said, "I can see that I'm going to have to keep my eye on you."

She reached a hand up to her heart. "Me? You think I trouble?"

"I'm certain of it."

She chuckled. "I not too bad trouble. You come at eleven o'clock with me and Rosa?"

Everything in her expression, her arched eyebrows and her widened eyes, which narrowed the longer I took to answer, told me she was about to get me into more trouble than I had ever known.

Chapter 8

At eleven o'clock sharp, just as I'd finished giving Lady a bath, Abuelita and Tia Rosa ushered me out of the restaurant.

Tia Rosa asked, "You drive?"

"I have a driver's license, but I haven't driven a car in two years." After my third fender-bender in a year, I had decided it was high time for me to take advantage of the excellent bike paths and public transportation system offered in Portland. It was cheaper than paying insurance.

"No problem. We still go," said Abuelita.

She crossed the street and turned down the block before I could ask where we were going. Then again, with Abuelita, the less I knew the better.

Tia Rosa tugged on my arm. "Let's go." She charged down the street after her sister enthusiastically.

Turning up a side street, we soon came to a

corner with bicycles piled outside shop doors. I loved riding bikes and the sight of them calmed my nerves. Maybe they simply wanted to go for a nice bike ride. I had noticed they both wore slacks, long-sleeved linen shirts, and sturdy shoes instead of their normal knee-length skirts, short sleeved blouses, and black leather heels.

Continuing down the street, my nerves gathered into a ball in my stomach when the bicycles thinned out and gave way to three-wheelers, dirt bikes, and quads. My palms started sweating when Abuelita and Tia Rosa entered a shop with four yellow dune buggies parked outside.

I followed them, afraid of what I'd hear but not wanting to miss a word.

Inside, a woman nursed her baby behind the cash register. Now, I have nothing against mothers feeding their babies in the way nature intended. However, most of the women I had seen breastfeeding in public wrapped a blanket or cover around them. This woman had nothing. I riveted my eyes to her face to keep from looking down — like a prude.

The woman greeted Abuelita and Tia Rosa by name, nodding at me and making another remark. Not having a clue what she was saying, I smiled and nodded politely as Tia Rosa patted my shoulder and said what I can only guess were nice things.

Thankfully, Tia Rosa didn't take long to translate. Nodding toward the woman I was still trying hard not to look at, she said, "She Miriam Proaño. She welcome you to Ecuador. Nice, eh?"

Smiling at Miriam, I said, "Gracias."

That seemed to be the correct thing to say, but it released a torrent of rapidly spoken words I could not even begin to try to comprehend. So I smiled and nodded some more. At least, I did until Abuelita smacked me across my midsection.

"Stop that. You look like tourist."

"I *am* a tourist," I retorted.

She huffed at me before resuming her amiable conversation with Miriam. She was the picture of charm, obviously wanting something. If the dune buggies were what she had in mind, she would have a rude awakening. I didn't know how to drive a stick shift. Not that I hadn't tried. My dad's attempt to teach me had ended in a series of visits to the chiropractor to align his neck.

Putting her hand out, Abuelita collected ten dollars from Tia Rosa, then motioned to me. "You have money? I pay for two hours. Is thirty dollar."

"Only if I don't have to drive that thing."

She didn't take me seriously. "Is easy. Little child drive buggy."

"Good, then you can do it." I knew I fought a losing battle, but she really had no idea what she asked of me.

Abuelita tossed the key at me and I fumbled to catch it. Perhaps if I had told her that I was quite possibly the world's worst driver — and that was saying a lot after Maria's white-knuckle ride from Quito — she wouldn't trust me with such a flimsy vehicle. It was no more than a roll cage with a motor!

"Can we get Jake to drive? Or Adi?" I begged.

"Jake work at office and Adi cook at restaurant. You drive us." Tia Rosa taped the bottom of her trousers and handed the roll over to Abuelita.

"Wait, this only seats two people. We won't fit. I'll stay here while you go wherever it is you're planning to go." It was the perfect solution.

Abuelita climbed into the passenger side. Tia Rosa did the same and, while they couldn't be comfortable sharing a seat like they were, they managed to buckle the seatbelt.

"We small," Tia Rosa said, squishing her sister to tap the steering wheel.

"I small. You fat," said Abuelita, shoving her shoulder over with her free hand.

"I don't know how to drive a dune buggy," I insisted.

"You drive car, you drive buggy. Come on. Is easy." Abuelita was losing patience with me.

"You don't understand. I'm a very bad driver."

She threw her arms up into the air. "No problem. Ecuador have many bad drivers. You with good company."

She had a point there.

All of my excuses spent, I ended with my most sincere argument, preparing myself for her cutting remark. "I'm scared." I clasped my hands in front of me, letting the key dangle from my fingers.

"Is because we no give you reason for brave." Tia Rosa's voice was apologetic, so when she tapped the driver seat beside her, I sat.

Placing her hand on top of mine, she continued, "I help you get bag."

Abuelita grunted. "*We* help you get bag. This my idea."

Perplexed, I asked, "What does this have to do with my backpack? As far as I know, my stuff is somewhere inside José's house. I ought to just go over there and ask him to return it."

"No! We no trust José. He bad man," Tia Rosa said.

"Then, I'll wait until the murder is solved and get my stuff from the police."

Abuelita scoffed. "You trust police solve murder? I no trust them. We solve murder, they return backpack."

She had a point. However, I wasn't eager to meddle in an investigation either. She still wasn't telling me everything.

"Where are we going that we can't walk or take a bus?"

Tia Rosa huffed. "José kill wife. He in love with Martha."

"What? How?" I had seen them in the same room together. He had paid more attention to his game than to her. I wasn't buying it.

Abuelita nodded her head resolutely. "Maria

mean sister. They no have children. Martha nice sister. Together, happy family."

"Not so happy if he murdered her sister." I didn't know why I was defending him, other than to be contrary. However, even I had to acknowledge how Martha's kids had crawled all over him. Clearly, they didn't fear him in the least. And Fernanda, the impossible-to-please teen, obviously loved her uncle. Not exactly the emotions a cold-blooded murderer would inspire in a pack of innocent kids.

"You no believe me," Abuelita accused. Waving her pointer finger in front of my nose and shoving her armpit into Tia Rosa's face in the process, she said in her normal feisty tone, "You know nothing about his business. José make puro from sugarcane. He grow plants in field of fathers."

I shrugged my shoulders, failing to understand how that made José a murderer. Besides, I already knew about his trade. Dario had told me.

"Maria killed with machete. José use machete to cut sugarcane. Police no find weapon. If we find machete in field, we solve murder."

"How do you know all that?" I asked. Fernanda had told me about the machete, but she hadn't said the murder weapon was lost. There were too many pieces missing, and every logical thought in my brain rebelled at Abuelita and Tia Rosa's suggestion. My lost backpack was merely an excuse for them to poke their noses where they didn't belong.

"We listen police. Cut to throat—" Not having the

words to describe the cut, Abuelita demonstrated by hacking her hand across Tia Rosa's throat and sliding her fingers across. Not the mental image I needed. A chill settled over me despite the midday heat of the afternoon.

"Police no find machete. It disappear," added Tia Rosa.

Their fallible reasoning aside, the first person I'd suspected was José. It was a sobering thought to realize I might have shaken hands with a violent murderer. I did not want to get involved. It would be the epitome of stupidity to go snooping around and potentially put our own lives in danger.

I moved a foot out of the buggy, ready to get out. I wanted nothing to do with this.

"I show you photograph of family. Thomas and Edison sweet boys. I have many photograph and Rosa have too."

My shoulders tensed. Thomas was my dad, and Edison was the uncle I only had one remaining memory of. She would use that against me. It was a manipulative trap. She couldn't know I'd never seen pictures of my uncle. He wasn't spoken about in our family. It was too painful.

Slowly, careful not to show how eager I was, I turned to face her, letting my foot dangle outside the door.

"You drive to Rio Negro. You help find machete. We tell you about brother of you father."

We stared at each other for a while, both of us as

determined as the other to get what she wanted. The problem was that I wanted to see a picture of a long-deceased uncle more than I wanted to stay out of Abuelita's crazy plan. What was wrong with me?

Before the sliver of sense I possessed could talk me out of it, I shoved the key into the ignition and fired up the dune buggy.

Chapter 9

We bunny hopped until the motor died. After two more tries, I finally found reverse. We hit the curb behind us so hard, it shot us forward and I ground the gear into first (or maybe it was third…) to take advantage of the momentum.

Peeking at my elderly accomplices, I said, "The gas pedal's a little touchy."

Tia Rosa grinned. "Step on it, Jess!"

Needing no further encouragement, I steered in the direction she pointed me. After weaving around traffic until I figured out the location of the brake, we made it somewhat safely onto the highway heading deeper into the jungle. Following the road, we wound around the curves carved in the mountainside, crossing the surging river, and passing a giant concrete dam with electricity towers surrounding it.

Abuelita signaled for me to pull over in a parking lot near the towers, so I did. She and Tia Rosa clambered out of their shared seat, stretched their limbs, then Tia Rosa reached into a plastic bag she had brought with her, pulling out three packets of those yellow plastic sheets people wore to Niagara Falls. It reminded me of the trip my family had taken to Disneyland during our winter vacation from school. The park had been crowded with tourists, and we had been delighted when it began raining because it meant that only the braver vacationers would wait in the lines. (After two days cramped together in our station wagon, we would have endured a tropical storm just to be outside.) Jessamyn, only four years old at the time, had thought the ponchos looked like daffodils.

Abuelita donned her plastic poncho and a pair of safety goggles, offering me another set she had packed. I gladly accepted the goggles, but I refused the poncho. As a proud Oregonian, I wasn't afraid of a little rain. Besides, it didn't look like it would rain with the clear skies above.

"You sure?" she asked, extending the daffodil with an insistent pulse of her hand.

"I'm sure," I said, pushing her offering aside.

Tia Rosa looked at her watch. "We no have much time. Let's go."

"Time for what? I know you paid for two hours, but we can always pay the extra if we're gone longer."

"No is money. Is time for lunch. José no work at lunch," she answered.

"How can you be sure of that?"

Cabs, Cakes, and Corpses

Abuelita grinned. "I send favorite food of José to Martha. Sylvia text me he with Martha." She patted her pocket where her cell phone must have been.

"If I'm in, then I'm all in." I would rather have been anywhere else than where we were for the reason we were there, but I craved to know more about my dad's twin. Uncle Eddy had let me pretend I was an airplane pilot. He'd plopped me on top of his shoulders and he'd ran around while I stretched my arms out and flew. That was the only vivid memory I had of him. It was a cool one, but it wasn't enough.

I pressed the throttle and we jolted forward. A bus honked at me and I stepped on the gas before it could run us over, forgetting that our top speed was half the speed limit.

The dune buggy didn't tip over on the sharp corners — a good thing because the bus driver rode our tail so closely, I had to take them quicker than I liked. At one point, I'm certain I could have reached back and touched the grill of the bus looming over us. Searching the narrow road for a place to pull over, we came upon a tunnel. Not exactly what I was looking for.

The two lanes of two-way traffic narrowed into a one lane as the highway split to go through the tunnel. I tried to turn on the headlights and immediately discovered that only one light worked. Enclosed in the dark, concrete tube, I opened the throttle as wide as it could go, knowing that it wasn't fast enough when the front of the bus tapped our buggy. Grasping the steering wheel as it fought to spin out of control, I heard Tia Rosa squealing in delight and Abuelita shaking her arm in the air and shouting at the bus driver. Scooting over as far as I could without scratching the paint on Abuelita's side of the buggy, I prayed the driver wouldn't be so stupid as to try to pass us in the narrow tunnel.

I had overestimated his intelligence. Closing my eyes and stomping on the brake to get it done quickly, I saw my life flash before my eyes. Was this how it was all going to end? In a dark tunnel in the middle of nowhere on the outskirts of the Amazon jungle?

I didn't know what to expect, having never been so close to death before, but it took a moment for me to understand that the light at the end of the tunnel was real. The lights flashing before my eyes weren't a collage of memories but, rather, the headlights of cars passing us. My hair swirled around my head and slapped me in the face.

Looking over at Abuelita and Tia Rosa, I asked, "Are you okay?"

Abuelita gave me a thumbs up.

Tia Rosa exclaimed, "That amazing! You great driver!"

My hands shook from the surge of adrenaline coursing through my body. Hopefully that was the only tunnel we would have to go through.

Just as my nerves began to relax, lulled into a false

Cabs, Cakes, and Corpses

sense of security by the buzz of the dune buggy engine, we came across another tunnel.

I held my breath and charged in. Not one hundred feet inside, I gasped as we drove into a wall of water. I tried to see through my goggles to the end of the tunnel. Windshield wipers would have been nice about now. Water crashed relentlessly down on us. We may as well have ridden a bicycle through a car wash.

Before I blindly ran into oncoming traffic, I tugged at the fogging goggles. The consuming darkness inside the tube and the water dropping like a series of cascades inside made it impossible to see. In my haste to rid myself of my goggles, they fell over the side. Squinting against the wind and moisture assaulting my face, I breathed a sigh of relief when I finally saw a growing pinpoint of daylight leading us outside.

Abuelita chattered next to me. She and Tia Rosa, of course, were cozy and dry underneath their yellow ponchos. Two dry daffodils. And one sopping idiot who had barely escaped from drowning.

A waterfall across the ravine distracted me from my self-disparaging thoughts. It fell down like a bride's veil, trailing through the rainbow midst until it met with the river.

Tia Rosa took a washcloth out of her plastic bag and wiped her goggles dry. "This place Rio Verde. Green River," she said. I wondered if Creedence Clearwater Revival knew about this place.

On the other side of Rio Verde, we drove through another tunnel just as wet as the one before. Had I known it was coming, I would've pulled over and accepted the rain gear from Abuelita. The stinker, who knew the roads so much better than I did, had not offered. She had the nerve to smile sweetly at me. I returned a glare.

Abuelita was saved from the tongue lashing I had rehearsed over and over in my mind when, on the other side of the tunnel, came a site that nearly took my breath away with its beauty. A stream of water poured down the side of the mountain. Surrounding it, the delicate flowers I had only ever seen in the finest flower shops poked out from the side of the rock. The high afternoon sun reflected off the stream of water, illuminating the colored blooms of the orchids and sparkling the midst like diamonds.

As we drove further down the mountain, the vegetation grew thicker. Leaves the size of an umbrella grew alongside the road. The insects were louder than the engine of our dune buggy. Having no protection against the elements, I tried to keep my mouth closed at the risk of swallowing a bug.

The next village, a tiny roadside town named San Francisco, had fruit stands with mandarins in mesh bags hanging above watermelons, passion fruit, papayas, and a variety of fruits I'd never seen. People sat in the shade in front of their houses and dozed in hammocks. Men pulled their shirts up to rub their bellies after their noon meal.

Cabs, Cakes, and Corpses

Abuelita tapped my arm, pointing out her side of the buggy. "You hungry?"

I was, in fact. Rather, I was until I saw what she pointed at. Along the side of the road, a large, pink pig hung. A tiny woman wielding a machete hacked off a section of it and threw it into a large pot over a fire.

I shouted over the sound of the motor and the bugs, "Does the dust add a particular flavor?"

Abuelita laughed. "You laugh now. By month end, you eat fritada."

"Fritada?"

"Fried pig meat."

Well, at least all of the bacteria would be cooked to death.

We drove on a few more minutes. The traffic slowed down, and I was able to really look around me. We must have descended quite a lot because the terrain flattened out. It was warmer too. A lot warmer. My cotton t-shirt dried and felt like stiff cardboard over my burning skin. So much for the fancy oil-free, non-comedogenic, broad spectrum SPF 60 Jessamyn had insisted would protect my skin without giving me breakouts. (It came highly recommended from the experts at Cosmo magazine and cost three times more than the cheap stuff I could have gotten at Wally World.)

On the bright side, I was grateful for the open vehicle in the absence of an air conditioner.

Abuelita slapped my arm with the back of her

hand while absently looking out her side of the buggy. "Slow down. Is close. We in Rio Negro. Black Water."

"No water. Is river. Black River," Tia Rosa corrected, leaving me to wonder if the Dooby Brothers had ever toured Ecuador with Creedence Clearwater Revival. The soundtrack of classic rock running through my head reminded me of my parents. They had excellent taste in music.

Abuelita pointed at a long trail off the side of the road. It was narrow and muddy from an earlier rain.

"Turn off light," she said with her finger over her lips.

"I can turn off the headlight, but there's nothing I can do about the sound of the motor." Why were we sneaking up on these people anyway? I almost made the mistake of asking her before remembering what we were searching for. Abuelita and Tia Rosa were convinced José had killed Maria and we were there to search for the murder weapon. We would not exactly be welcome company.

The heat was stifling. The sugarcane growing on either side of the road closed in around us and brushed against the sides of our dune buggy. My apprehension grew as the path narrowed. Snooping around someone's property, hoping that we wouldn't get caught was not an everyday activity for me. I mean, I'm the kind of person who feels a surge of rebellion when I walk in the exit at the grocery store or return a library book one day after it's due. Call me boring, but I have always walked on the safe side of the law — unlike the two ladies beside me.

Filled with terror and a tiny ration of excitement, I followed Abuelita's orders, reminding myself of what she had promised me. It would be worth it, I reminded myself over and over.

"Turn off buggy," she said as a small, cement block house came into view. It couldn't have had more than one room, but a giant window faced the path we were trying to sneak in on. We could see inside the house as clearly as they could see out. An elderly couple sat at a table in front of their curtain-less window, pouring from a two-liter bottle of Coca Cola and eating something off of a plate. We would have to go right by them.

Hiding behind the tall sugarcane, we got out of our buggy to peek around and investigate our surroundings. We were surrounded by the thick stalks of grass. The only opening was the clearing where the small house was.

"They José's parents," Tia Rosa said, confirming what I suspected.

I was new to this cloak and dagger stuff, but even I knew that we could not keep our dune buggy parked in the middle of the narrow lane. Looking around for a place to hide the buggy, I found a narrow path where the sugarcane was shorter than the rest. It looked just wide enough to stash our transportation until we were ready to leave. So long as no one else came down the lane, it shouldn't draw attention.

The muddy road made the work difficult, but the ladies helped me push it out of the path, backing it into the spot to better make a quick exit.

My fingers had swollen up to the size of sausages, and my feet felt tight inside my sneakers. I pulled my stiff clothes away from me, the damp denim of my jeans clinging to and chafing against my skin.

Turning to Abuelita, I asked, "Which fields do we search?" I prayed she would know exactly which area to look in. Otherwise, we would be there until nightfall searching in the dark for a machete we would still have difficulty proving José had used to killed Maria.

Abuelita plopped her hands on her hips, looking ready to take on the sugarcane.

"All this," she waved her arm around us in a circle, "belong José. We start behind house. Look for place he make puro."

It was going to be a long afternoon.

Keeping as close to the grass as I could, we crept past the house. I knew they couldn't hear me, but I still held my breath as we walked by.

The river rumbled as we got closer to the water and I looked longingly at the shade the trees offered on its bank.

However, shade was not in my foreseeable future. Abuelita dove into the sugarcane, her eyes trained on the ground for any sign of a bloody machete. Tia Rosa waded through the grass further down. I followed her, looking in the opposite direction from her in a hopeful, albeit futile, attempt to shorten our time in the fields. I tripped over something, lunging forward and smacking Tia Rosa against the back.

"I'm sorry," I whispered.

Tia Rosa spun around, investigating the ground at my feet. Looking back up at me, she said, "Is only root of tree. Be careful for snake."

I felt the blood drain from my body and my arms fell limply at my sides. "There are snakes out here?" I asked.

Tia Rosa clucked her tongue and shook her head. "We in jungle. We by river. Anaconda live in river. Boa constrictor live in jungle."

Fabulous.

Chapter 10

I had seen movies set in the jungle, but it hadn't truly dawned on me until that moment that the creatures added to the scenes for extra drama could actually be in the sugarcane field we were searching through. Please let anacondas be nocturnal. I had seen part of a documentary about the gigantic, man-eating snake — wait, could an anaconda really swallow a man whole? I asked Tia Rosa.

"National Geographic say they no can, but my eyes see it."

I imagined she saw a lot with her pink, magnifying spectacles.

She continued, "He stupid man. Small man. He drink too much and walk alone in jungle. Estúpido."

Not completely unlike what we were doing. At least the man had the excuse of being drunk. We were supposedly intelligent females who chose to traipse around in fields where wild animals could eat us.

Cabs, Cakes, and Corpses

Deciding to end our search as rapidly as possible, I kept my questions to myself (they didn't get good answers anyway) and covered a large area in short time searching for José's machete.

Only stopping to slap the mosquitoes and assorted bugs away from me, I dove through the layers of grass, feeling my skin blister and my forehead burn.

I would be a pretty sight when we got back to Baños. I brushed my swollen hands down my arms and legs. I couldn't see them yet, but I could feel the itchy bumps covering my exposed skin and crawling inside my pant legs. Now I knew why the grannies had taped their long slacks and had worn long-sleeved shirts. They probably had the presence of mind to put some bug juice on before we left. I hadn't.

The field ended abruptly and we found ourselves standing in the middle of a clearing. A crooked wooden shed as big as José's parent's concrete house sat directly in front of us. It had a tin roof and a chimney. An odd sight in a place so warm.

Abuelita charged forward to it. "Is distillery," she said excitedly.

"Is distillery!" a voice repeated. "Distillery!" another voice added. I looked around in panic. We were surrounded, but Abuelita didn't try to hide and Tia Rosa chuckled at me.

"Is parrots," she explained, pointing to the trees by the river. "We talk quiet or they blow cover."

"Blow cover?" I chose to be more impressed at her

use of an English idiom than embarrassed at being scared by talkative parrots.

"I watch movie with subtitle. Drive Bertha crazy, but I learn." Tia Rosa stepped out from the grass, signaling for me to follow.

I was thrilled to get out of the grass. The bugs were eating me alive and I hoped we would find what we searched for in the small building so we could go back to civilization, food that wouldn't kill me, hot showers, and gobs of aloe vera lotion in the safety of Adi's apartment.

A large padlock closed the peeling plywood doors. Searching in her pocket, Abuelita pulled out a bobby pin and worked on the lock. Evidently, she was no stranger to breaking and entering.

Not wanting to stand around useless, I circled the building. Warped panels of wooden sheets with nails poking out of them haphazardly covered the sides. If the Big Bad Wolf blew on it, the whole thing would fall down … Which gave me an idea.

I pulled on a panel, shouting softly in triumph when it came off in my hands. "Got it!" Setting it against the shed, I opened my mouth to call for Abuelita and Tia Rosa to join me, but the parrots beat me to it.

"Got it!" echoed through the fields. There must have been half a dozen parrots repeating me.

Tia Rosa clapped her hands when she saw what I had done. In a low whisper, she said, "Well done, Jess. You a smart girl."

Cabs, Cakes, and Corpses

"She too loud," complained Abuelita.

I ignored Abuelita. The praise was nicer, even considering her reason for giving it — assisting her in a fanciful search on private property where we would no doubt be thrown into jail if we were caught. Her words would give me no end of comfort as I languished in a dreary jail cell. And all so I could look at some old pictures. Suddenly, I didn't feel so smart.

Bowled over by the smell, I almost fell into a horse trough filled with what looked like bubbling, popping sewage waste. Oranges floated on top of the steaming concoction covered with mesh to keep out the bugs. I waved a path through the flies hovering around the vile liquid and the grinder next to it. Stalks of cut sugarcane rested against the metal grinder.

"He make the puro here," said Abuelita as she pushed past me, moving to the opposite end of the room. A tank as tall as her hovered over a fire pit. A copper still with a mess of straight and coiled tubes running into gas containers clearly identified the room as a distillery. My nostrils burned.

Tia Rosa wandered to the back of the room. "Why he have this? Is no puro." A wash tub with a brown liquid smelling of black licorice and cinnamon sat in front of a shelf lined with empty, glass liquor and plastic Sprite bottles. The labels had been peeled off of the glass bottles, but I still recognized them. Johnny Walker whiskey, Smirnoff vodka, and Antioqueño aguardiente. They stood in stark contrast to the cheap plastic next to them.

I continued searching around the room, determined that if I was going to be caught searching where I was unwelcome, at least I would do a thorough job of it.

Sheets of plywood leaned against the wall by the distillery. Replacement boards for the outer walls? So much for security. It made the giant padlock outside the front doors seem pointless.

I stubbed my toes against a tree trunk next to the front doors of the shed. Abuelita stared at it with her arms crossed, clucking her tongue.

"Is no here." She pointed at the tree stump.

I looked closer at the top of the stump and saw what she meant. Hundreds of slices cut into the wood in a sort of rustic knife block. If the machete was anywhere to be found, it would have been there.

Tia Rosa, holding her hand over her mouth and nose, ducked out of the shed. Good idea. The smell of fermenting sugarcane was overpowering.

Turning to Abuelita to suggest we leave as well, I froze in place when someone outside tugged on the padlock. The shed trembled, and my heart leapt into my throat.

Abuelita reacted instantly, dashing for the opening at the side of the shed. I hesitated. That was my big mistake.

I heard the click of the lock open. There wasn't enough time to cross the room and replace the siding without being seen. Diving headfirst behind the stash of plywood, I crouched down on the dirt floor, making myself as small as I could when the doors opened and I heard footsteps come inside. Had I thought things through quicker, I would have faced myself in the opposite direction. As it was, I could see nothing.

My breath thundered in my ears. If my heart beat any louder, it would give me away. Something crawled against my hand and I had to bite my lips together not to scream. Shaking my fingers, a flurry of wings attacked my face. Not having any other option, I closed my eyes and scrunched my face up hoping it was a harmless butterfly and not some giant, blood-sucking bug.

I had no idea how much time passed, my battle with the flying bugs and my struggle to remain quiet distracting me too much. The footsteps and rustling stopped and a dead silence filled the room. Uh oh.

Tightening myself into a ball, I strained my ears to listen. A man exclaimed unhappily, and I didn't have to understand him to know that he had found the open panel on the side of his shed. I just hoped he didn't see Abuelita or Tia Rosa ... wherever they were.

A chorus of voices called, "Hijito, a comer!" With a sigh loud enough for me to hear, and a thump behind me, the man walked away from me, the sound of his footsteps fading.

I crawled forward so I could peek through the gap between the boards in the shelving. The shed was empty.

Losing no time, I backed out as quickly as I could, falling back against the stump and smacking my head against José's machete. That had been the thump! Without stopping to think, I grabbed the machete, pinching it between my thumb and finger so as not to ruin any prints or DNA samples or whatever they might have needed from a murder weapon, wishing I had had the sense to wear gloves to keep my fingerprints off of it. Oh well, there was no time. Darting for the tall grass, I ran past the house and toward the space where I had parked the dune buggy. Abuelita came up behind me, running faster than I had ever seen a woman in her sixties run. She was fit. Tia Rosa hobbled a few paces behind her, her round face gleaming with sweat.

Climbing into our vehicle, which José was sure to have seen, I stuffed his machete between the seats, shoved the key into the ignition, and slammed my foot on the gas pedal, leaving a spray of mud behind me.

Worried more about getting caught by the people behind us than the drivers on the road in front of us, we burst out from the trail and onto the main highway. Horns and squealing tires surrounded us, but the scream echoing in my own ears was louder.

Maneuvering between cars much larger than ours, I eventually got in the correct lane and, without a look back, I pressed down on the gas pedal only to find out that it was already pressed to the floor. *And the award for the world's worst driver officially goes to Jessica James*, I thought, looking over at my partners in

Cabs, Cakes, and Corpses

crime. I saw the fleeting look of concern leave Tia Rosa's face as she smiled bravely at me. It served her and Abuelita right for dragging me out here. They had been warned. Of course, I was particularly cautious for the rest of the drive home, not once allowing my thoughts to wander or to take my hands off the steering wheel to scratch one of the thousands of bug bites covering my blistered, sunburned body.

We passed through three tunnels before my limbs stopped shaking and my heartbeat stopped pounding like a ticking bomb.

"Thank you for helping me escape," I said. "What did you do?"

Tia Rosa cackled. "We pretend be mother of José. We call him for eat lunch. The parrots repeat."

"Brilliant!" I laughed a little too heartily. It must have been the nerves.

"And you find machete." Abuelita nodded toward the sharp instrument vibrating with the roar of the motor between the seats.

"That wasn't all I found." The bottles. While I understood that making moonshine was a common and oftentimes legal activity — I seriously doubted the legality of José's operation — the brand name liquor bottles were definitely out of place. And the tub of spiced water? He certainly didn't add that to his crystal-clear puro.

"What can José be doing with all of those bottles? I saw whiskey, aguardiente, and vodka bottles in his shed. The same bottles he had with him on the plane."

"Is problem in Ecuador. Tax for good liquor very expensive. If José find way to fake good liquor, he make fortune," said Abuelita.

Tia Rosa nodded. "It explain new taxi car."

"We go to The Lava Lounge tonight," Abuelita declared. "If José do business with Dario, it explain everything."

"Oh no! I am done investigating. We could have been caught, and I don't much like the idea of going to jail in a foreign country."

Abuelita clucked her tongue. "You no think that before you take machete of José?"

I cringed. She was right. Like it or not, he would notice it was gone and I couldn't exactly give it to the police with my fingerprints all over it. They would ask how I'd found it. We would be admitting to trespassing, breaking and entering, vandalism (although that was a stretch considering how poorly the shed was constructed), and who knew what other charges....

And if José had really murdered his wife, as I was growing more inclined to think, there would be nothing to stop him from going after us. We knew his secret.

Chapter 11

Miriam wasn't too happy about the state of her dune buggy when we returned it, but a couple of dollars kept us from having to stay and wash the mud caked onto its frame. I was relieved. All I wanted was to get home, clean up, and ask Abuelita questions about my uncle before going to the pub with Adi and Jake.

As usual, the streets were busy and, with the way that people turned to look at me, I must have provided quite the site. I avoided looking at my reflection in the shop windows we passed. Sometimes ignorance really was bliss.

Lady greeted us when we entered from the gate. She spun in a circle and pounced on her front feet excitedly. Picking up one of the chew toys I'd bought her, I threw it for her to chase. I would need to take her out for a walk tomorrow.

Abuelita and Tia Rosa took off her plastic

ponchos. Smoothing out their slacks, running their hands over her faces, and fluffing their hair, they looked none the worse for wear. Unlike me. I felt like I'd crawled out of a swamp....

The ladies breezed into the kitchen, kissing Adi and Sylvia on the cheeks. I stopped after one step into the kitchen, not wanting to contaminate the room. I still felt things crawling on my skin and my legs were swollen to twice their normal size with bubbled, itchy bites.

Adi almost dropped the plate she held when she finally noticed me. "Oh my God," she said, her eyes as large as saucers.

Sylvia's eyes also widened in shock when she saw me, before narrowing to focus on her mother, who had been very affectionate and attentive to them since entering the room.

"What did you do to her?" asked Sylvia.

Abuelita shrugged her shoulders, doing her best imitation of an innocent, sweet, old lady. "We go nice drive to Rio Negro. Jessica a wonderful driver," she smiled. The liar.

Undeterred, she continued, "She see waterfalls and we walk, but Jessica too sweet. The bugs, they love her."

While Abuelita's acting skills were worthy of an Oscar, I could see from Adi and Sylvia's expressions that they didn't believe her. Tia Rosa remained suspiciously quiet.

"What? Didn't you use the trails or the cable cars

to get across?" asked Adi, crossing her arms over her apron.

Sylvia wrapped her arm around my shoulders and tucked a chunk of hair behind my ear. "What you need is a good shower in very hot water. I will go to the pharmacy and ask if they can give you an anti-inflammatory to help the swelling and a cream to alleviate the itching."

"You can do that? Don't you need a prescription from a doctor for pills?" I asked, feeling naive as I was met with their blank stares.

Adi laughed. "Not here. If you need something at the pharmacy, you just ask for it."

"Seriously?"

"Seriously," said Sylvia, adding, "I forget how difficult it is with doctors and insurance and all that nonsense." She waved her hand dismissively to emphasize her feelings on the subject. "I will be back soon with something to help you."

That sounded wonderful. I would've preferred to go myself, but I wouldn't know how to ask for what I needed and I was too miserable to go even if I did.

Before Sylvia could leave, I asked if anyone had called to claim Lady. We had agreed that the best phone number to put on the posters Adi and I had taped around town was the restaurant's.

Sylvia answered, "I've been here all day and nobody has called for her."

It was sad how someone could forget the cute puppy, but I was relieved she wouldn't have to go back to a family who didn't even care if she was gone or not.

Pulling off her apron and hanging it on a peg by the door, Sylvia said, "Before I forget, Agent Vasquez called for you. He did not sound happy, but then again, I doubt he ever does. I wouldn't worry about it. I told him I didn't know at what hour to expect you home, so he told me that he would stop by later." With that, she disappeared behind the swinging door.

Great. Just great. I can only imagine what Agent Vasquez would say if he found out about our escapade through José's sugarcane field. Already, I was thinking of good places to hide his machete. A couple days with Abuelita and Tia Rosa, and they had me thinking like a criminal.

Grumbling all the way upstairs, I turned on the faucet and waited for the bathroom to fill up with steam. No more cold showers for me. It was amazing how even in the warm, tropical climate, I still craved a hot shower.

For a while, I just stood under the flowing water, letting it pound against my back. It felt so good. I hadn't realized how tense the muscles in my neck and upper back were until they relaxed.

Though I had to admit there were parts of Baños which had won me over, I still couldn't wait to get back home. A week's visit would have been sufficient, but my parents had never done anything halfheartedly. It would be a long month.

I thought back on the scene in Martha's house. I

felt bad for Fernanda. While her manners and indifference had made me wonder if she could have killed her own aunt to bring her mom and uncle together, I couldn't believe she'd actually done it. It was nothing more than a gut feeling, but for some reason, I wanted to like Fernanda. Maybe her harsh exterior was an act to cover her sadness? Her affection for her uncle made her blind. He was up to no good and, as the evidence against him piled up, I had to agree he knew more about Maria's death than he let on. Him and Dario. That man gave me the creeps.

Reaching up through the thick steam, I fumbled for the shampoo. Something fuzzy squirmed under my fingers. Panic seized me, but that didn't prevent me from screaming when my eyes focused on the biggest spider I had ever seen.

Not knowing what to do with the giant creature, we stood and stared at each other. It was too big to squish and the only advice that came to mind was an old memory of a road trip I had taken with my mom and dad to Yellowstone National Park. We were told not to panic or run if we saw a bear. Unfortunately, that was all I could remember and I doubted it applied to arachnids. Would the spider attack if I made any sudden movements?

There was a loud bang on my front door, and I heard Adi shouting, "Jess, are you okay?"

"There's an enormous spider in here. I touched it!"

"I'll be right back. I don't do spiders."

Well, I didn't do spiders either. I could only guess who she was getting, and I prayed it would be anyone but Jake. A guy could only save a girl so many times in the shower.

Slowly, very slowly, I reached up to slide my towel off the rod of the shower curtain. Wrapping it around me, I waited as close to the opposite wall as I could from the hairy creature. I couldn't even turn off the water, the faucet being much too close to the tarantula.

Jake knocked on the bathroom door. "Are you decent?"

I wanted to laugh. It was either that or die of mortification. If bathing wasn't a necessary daily activity (especially in this sticky climate) I would have considered giving up the activity until my return to Portland and my insect-free shower. "I'm fine, but I don't know what to do about the spider sharing my shower."

Jake opened the door and pulled aside the shower curtain. Turning off the water and covering the tarantula with a hand towel in one swift motion, he gathered the edges of the towel like a little bag that carried nothing I ever wanted to see again inside it.

Holding the bagged spider up in a salute, he laughed. "This is becoming a habit."

"Next time, I'll wear a bathing suit."

"Clever idea." Jake backed toward the door. "By the way, Agent Vasquez is waiting for you downstairs."

I peeked around the curtain to make sure Jake had gone and had taken the furry monster with him.

Bracing myself for the inevitable, I made short time of dressing and combing my hair. I didn't bother to put on any makeup. My face was so burned, it hurt to touch.

Lady gnawed on a bone at the bottom of the steps. As hungrily as she chewed on her treat, she dropped it and stood as I passed.

"It's okay, girl. You need to eat," I encouraged her, pointing to her bone. It was like she understood me, because once I gave her permission and a scratch behind the ears, she dedicated her full attention to the bone once again. What a cool dog. I'd be very sad when it was time to leave her.

Sylvia greeted me at the kitchen door with a little, plastic pharmacy bag full of pills and cream.

Holding out a glass of water and two pills, she said, "The white one is an anti-inflammatory and the little yellow one is an antihistamine. The pharmacist recommended you take both every twelve hours until your symptoms improve."

I popped them in my mouth, chasing them down with a gulp of cool water.

"Thank you. I don't think I've ever burned myself this badly."

"It's the altitude. We should have thought to warn you." Sylvia's cheeks bunched up and she huffed her disappointment. As if it was her fault. It was the same expression my mom wore when she assumed responsibility for someone else's mistake.

"We can reschedule our pub night, Jess. You look like you feel miserable," said Adi.

What a relief to be able to spend a night in. And better still, no one had mentioned the shower episode.

With an impish grin and mischievous arch of her eyebrow, Adi asked, "How was your shower?"

So much for that! "Interesting. I hope it's the last time I get an unwelcome guest in the shower."

Adi giggled. "To whom do you refer? Jake or the spider?"

As if I wasn't red enough, I felt my face blush.

Abuelita smacked me across the arm. She did that a lot. "You lucky girl. Many woman try get Jake in shower, and he see you two time!" Her whole body shook as she cackled with Tia Rosa.

Still laughing, Adi grabbed a kitchen towel and ran it under the faucet, wringing the excess water out before tossing it to me. "Here, this will cool you down," she said.

I gladly buried my face in the cloth until Sylvia reminded me that Agent Vasquez waited in the dining room. Oh, the joy.

Chapter 12

I grabbed Abuelita's hand. "Come with me," I said, knowing she would be a much better liar then me if he asked questions I didn't want to answer.

"He no like me. I try for you."

Together, we walked to Agent Vasquez's table in a corner offering some privacy from the diners. He stood when we joined him. Motioning to the seat opposite him, he said, "Please have a seat, Miss James." To Abuelita, he said, "Thank you, Mrs. Jimenez. That will be all," dismissing her before she could take a seat.

Squeezing my hand before she left, I begrudgingly sat in the chair he offered me.

"Where were you this afternoon?"

He knew how to get to the point.

I shifted my weight on my chair. It was impossible to sit comfortably with so many bites.

"Abuelita and Tia Rosa, the Missus Jimenez, took me to see the waterfalls. They were beautiful, and I'd like to go again. Which is your favorite?"

The wood squeaked as Agent Vasquez sat back against his chair, looking at me dead on. "Really?"

I nodded and smiled feebly.

He crossed his arms. "How did you get there?"

I was unfamiliar with licensing laws in Ecuador, but I was pretty sure it was illegal to drive a dune buggy on a major highway. I hadn't seen any others about. Maybe if I played the 'ignorant tourist' card, he'd let me off with a warning. I tried to breathe normally and hold my hands still, though the urge to pop my knuckles was unbearable.

"We crammed into a dune buggy. I'd never driven one before, but once I got the hang of it, I really enjoyed it." I grinned, feeling the skin on my cheeks crack.

"I'm guessing it wasn't a planned trip?"

"It was a surprise. Otherwise, I would have worn sunscreen and bug repellent."

He sat forward, clasping his hands on top of the table. "Hmm," he grunted, narrowing his eyes at me and drawing all sorts of conclusions. I could only hope they were favorable.

After an eternity, he smiled. "Those are fun. Did you stick to the road or take the bike paths?" He almost seemed like a normal man and not a scary detective. Or was this some variation of "Good Cop/Bad Cop"?

Cabs, Cakes, and Corpses

I hadn't recalled seeing any bike paths. Of course, the path leading to José's fields could qualify. "We mostly stuck to the road, but we did take some paths." It was the truth. Mostly.

He considered me for a while, clearly trying to determine whether or not I told the truth. Finally, he leaned forward over his clasped hands and lowered his voice. "Miss James, do you know why I requested this interview today?"

Another honest answer. "No, I don't. Unless you have caught the murderer and you have come to return my backpack," I said hopefully.

He crushed my hopes in one bluntly spoken word. "No. I asked José and he didn't recall seeing it. He assured me it wasn't in his house."

I sighed, feeling my shoulders hunch over ever so slightly. I knew Agent Vasquez had much worse problems to deal with than tracking down my bag, but I still mourned its loss. "Oh, well, thank you for asking. I appreciate it. The folks at Casa Hood were nice enough to let me borrow some books and I can start a new journal until I can replace it when I get home." I closed my mouth. Agent Vasquez's patience thinned the more I rambled. "Sorry. Why did you want to talk to me?"

"I received a disturbing call from Señor Guzmán." He paused, letting his words sink in. And sink in they did. My legs started fidgeting. I put my hands over them to still them, saying, "Too much coffee," in a lame excuse to disguise my nerves. I would never be able to trick a lie detector test. He probably saw right through me.

Agent Vasquez observed me silently, making me more nervous with each passing second. I wished he'd say something.

Needing to fill the silence, I asked, "Is José okay?"

"I don't know. You tell me."

I channeled my inner Abuelita and shrugged my shoulders as nonchalantly as I could. I drew the line at poking him in the chest though. I didn't think he'd react well to that. "Why would I know? I haven't seen him."

Now, technically, that was absolutely true. Though I was certain it had been him inside the shed, I hadn't seen him with my eyes.

"Is that so? How interesting." He stared at me as if he could read the truth in my eyes. There was a reason I always got into trouble while my sisters got off scot-free. Even when I was absolutely innocent, they had a way of blaming me in such a way that made me look completely guilty. You'd think that as an adult, I would've had a clue, but as I sat there under his scrutinizing stare, I realized he was doing exactly what they did. And it made me mad.

Straightening my shoulders and sticking both of my feet to the floor to keep from fidgeting, I repeated over and over in my head, 'I did not see José.' Looking Agent Vasquez squarely in the face, I said again, "I have not seen José since the morning his wife was killed. If there is any way you think I may be of assistance to you in your investigation, please tell me so I can help. Otherwise, I do not understand why you are here if it is not to return my things to me." The self-possession in my voice surprised me.

I would not allow him to treat me like a suspect when I knew I was innocent.

The corner of his thin lips twitched. "How did you get so many bites?" he asked.

"I'm too sweet."

His gaze narrowed at me, but I didn't waver. I was on a roll of confidence, and I wasn't ready to get off that particular train just yet.

"It's most uncommon even for fresh blood to get that many bites unless your traipsing out in a place with a lot of vegetation ... say, a sugarcane field?"

I swallowed hard, but I held steady. If he sought proof, he was not going to get it from me.

He continued, "Is there anything you want to tell me, Miss James?"

No. Definitely, no.

We sat in silence, staring at each other in a stalemate. I wouldn't give, and he couldn't attack unless I did. I knew it and he seemed to know it too.

"The first of our samples from the crime scene came back...." He let the rest of his sentence trail off unspoken.

The butterflies in my stomach fluttered nervously, but I kept them in check. "That's good. I hope you find the murderer." I really did hope that. I knew my DNA must've been all over the backseat of the car, but surely he knew why, right? The way he stared at me made me wonder.

"How long have you known Mrs. Jimenez?"

My breath caught in my throat. "Which one?" I whispered, trying to gather my thoughts.

"Have you known one longer than the other?" he asked incredulously.

My throat felt dry, but I squeaked out, "I hadn't met the Jimenez family before arriving here yesterday. They have, however, been good friends of my parents for many years."

I clasped my fingers together so I couldn't fiddle my fingers.

"And what is your opinion of the señoras Jimenez?"

I knew my answer was important from the way he looked at me, which had the undesired effect of clearing my mind of all rational intelligence.

"That is an excellent question and it deserves a thoughtful answer," I said, my mind reeling while I stalled for time. I allowed myself a moment to gather my thoughts under the observing eye of Agent Vasquez. As always happened, just at the peak of my inhale, something clicked. Whatever Agent Vasquez had discovered or believed to be true, I knew in my heart that none of us in the restaurant were in any way responsible for the death of Maria Guzmán. I had no cause to be nervous, nor any reason for my confidence to fail me because the truth was on my side. That had to count for something. I knew what to say.

"There is a reason why everyone in town calls them Abuelita and Tia. Did you know they sent enough food to feed Martha's entire family today — and plan to continue to do so for the rest of the week? Abuelita has a strong personality and Tia Rosa comes across as oblivious, but actions such as these show that they have a strong sense of values, of right and wrong, of humanity, and decency. If they have involved themselves in your investigation, it was done to protect their friends in a time of need. Everyone should have such a loyal friend as Abuelita and Tia Rosa." More than ever, I was relieved to have those crazy ladies on my side.

Agent Vasquez looked at me askance. "You've learned all this in a day and a half?"

Indeed. "It's been busy." It felt like a lifetime had passed since I'd boarded my first airplane in Portland.

Agent Vasquez nodded. "I thought you would answer as much, and let me warn you about your new friends. To me, the Jimenez sisters appear to be nothing more than accomplished con artists who make themselves likable to suit their purpose. You should know that the woman you call Tia Rosa is the chief suspect in the murder of Maria Guzmán, and your association with her doesn't reflect well on you."

"What proof do you have?" I asked, keeping my cool. Agent Vasquez didn't know it, but the table had turned. I needed information, and he was going to provide it.

Chapter 13

Agent Vasquez said nothing. Had he heard me?

"If I am to believe your allegations, I need facts. Why is Tia Rosa under suspicion?" Calm down, lassie. Too bitey. He wouldn't share anything with me like that. I needed to be a victim.

Relaxing my eyebrows, widening my eyes, and slumping my shoulders, I raised my hand up to my forehead and let my elbow rest against the table, shaking my head as the realization settled in that I may have been duped. (At least, that's what I wanted him to think.) I added breathlessly, "They are such nice, old ladies." Okay, maybe that was stretching it a bit, but I needed him to feel sorry for poor, little, foolish me.

It worked.

"I will give you what facts pertain to your situation in the expectation that you cut all ties with the señoras Jimenez. By Señora Rosa's own testimony, she had not seen María Guzmán the day of her murder or the day before. It is a blatant lie."

"A lie? I don't understand...." I considered twirling a piece of hair, but decided against it. I wanted him to think I was merely dumbfounded, not a complete bimbo.

I shrugged. "Maybe she forgot. That's hardly incriminating evidence."

"Senora Jimenez's fingerprints were on the driver's side of the cab at the crime scene."

I shook my head, fishing for more. "She may have taken her taxi during the week. There must be hundreds of prints all over the car."

"Her prints were fresh. No smudges to indicate they had been made days before."

Okay, now I was starting to get worried. "You said they were on the front of the car? How many people really rest their fingers on the front of the car? Couldn't they have been made days ago?"

His eyebrows raised. "How can you explain the curly, gray hair on the hood of the car Señora Guzmán was slain in?"

He raised his hand. "Before you suggest that somehow some adhesive material on the hood of her car prevented the hair from blowing away, let me stop you. The fingerprints and the hair put Señora Rosa at the scene of the crime within the time frame of the murder."

"You can't honestly think she did it." No matter how hard I tried, I couldn't even imagine Tia Rosa wielding a machete. There wasn't a mean bone in her squishy body.

"At this point, I have to consider everyone a suspect. It's my job. And I'm very good at it."

I wasn't ready to let it go just yet. "Why would she go to Maria's house to get my stuff if she had just murdered her? Wouldn't she want to stay away? I was with her when we went to give our condolences to the family as soon as we learned what had happened."

"Can you account for her presence the *entire* time?" he asked.

No, no, sir. You are not going to get information from me.

Choosing my words quickly, I let my nerves loose. I fidgeted and avoided eye contact.

"What? What do you remember?" he asked, leaning forward, his pen poised over a notepad.

"Um. Well…" I finally met his gaze and wrinkled my forehead in consternation. Just when I thought he'd burst with impatience, I said, "I feel so foolish now, but maybe I should have followed her into the bathroom. I don't think she would have appreciated that, but—"

He raised his hand, his cheeks bunched up in disappointment or disgust. "That was not necessary."

I congratulated myself at avoiding his question successfully.

"However, your willingness to follow her leads me to believe you capable of going with her to José's shed this afternoon."

Well, that had backfired.

"Me?" I asked, convinced he saw through my innocent front. For years, it hadn't fooled Mom either. It must be I was out of practice.

"You could only have two reasons for pulling such a stupid stunt." He raised one thick finger. "You were attempting to plant evidence against José for the murder of his wife. My men are searching the fields as we speak for the weapon used to kill Señora Guzmán."

Agent Vasquez kept his cards close to his chest, but I knew what weapon they searched for. A machete. I also knew they would not find it. I had José's machete. Unlike Abuelita, I wasn't convinced José had used that particular machete to kill his wife, but it had my fingerprints all over it.

He held up another finger and I readied myself to hear stupid reason number two. "The only other explanation and, by far the more foolish of the two, is in an effort to retrieve your backpack, you have involved yourselves in a murder case in which you have no right to poke your noses. Your impatience and interference are impediments to my investigation."

It was difficult for me to take his dig seriously when it was so well alliterated. "It never was my intent to interfere, impede, or unintentionally invoke inconvenience in your investigation."

"You may not think it's so humorous when you miss your flight home. That's right, Miss James, if your actions cause me to take longer than normal to wrap up this case, I'll make you stay for the trial as a key witness."

"Inconceivable," I mumbled, feeling as smart as Vizzini right before he keeled over.

"Believe me, I'll do it if you continue to hinder my progress."

I didn't have to pretend to look shocked. Making a mental note not to underestimate Agent Vasquez, I listened as he continued.

"I am going out to José's distillery right now. I wonder what evidence I'll find against you there…."

His threats effectively delivered, Agent Vasquez placed his notepad in the pocket of his black polo shirt, downed the last of the water in his glass, and sauntered out to his black SUV with the tinted windows sitting at the side of the park full of carefree tourists. Unlike them, I was very soon to be in a great deal of trouble and my conscience tormented me at involving Tia Rosa and Abuelita. I shouldn't have made such a big deal about losing my bag… as if I couldn't handle life without books and cinnamon gum. It had seemed important at the time, but it wasn't worth going to jail over.

Bracing my hands against the table, I stood, my resolve in pursuing my new goal as firm as a bulldog's bite. I had a murderer to catch.

Four sets of inquisitive eyes landed on me as I returned to the kitchen.

Sylvia spoke first, setting aside her knife and the

mound of onions and bell peppers waiting to be chopped. "What did Agent Vasquez want?"

I looked over at Abuelita and Tia Rosa, who leaned against the side of the island.

"I know what he want," Tia Rosa said, the resignation in her voice adding to my resolve to clear her name.

Before she could continue, I asked her, "I thought you said you left no evidence behind you, but Agent Vasquez just told me he lifted your prints from Maria's car. How did that happen?"

Abuelita crossed her arms and shook her head. "Is estúpido."

Tia Rosa came over to me, reaching up to pat my shoulder. "Bertha right. Is stupid. We make bad choice."

"Why did you lie to me about it? I was defenseless out there."

She patted my cheek. "I no worry you, okay? Is no problem."

Adi wrapped her arms around Tia Rosa's open side. "It doesn't sound like it's no problem."

Abuelita lifted her head defiantly. "Is my fault. My idea, it bad."

Sylvia stepped toward Abuelita. "Mother, what have you been doing?"

Abuelita didn't seem to want to tell her daughter what she had done, so I did. "When we went over to get my bag and found out Maria had been murdered, Abuelita and Tia Rosa pretended to go to the bathroom. What they really did was climb over the property wall into the Guzmán's garage in an attempt to get my stuff back for me. If only I'd been more patient. I didn't know—"

"You stop!" interrupted Abuelita. "I make decision. Rosa make decision. You no fault."

"But I really did want my stuff back and I think I made too much of a big deal about it."

Tia Rosa put her hand over my mouth. "I mature woman. I make choice. I pay consequence. How you be guilty for my choice?" She clucked her tongue at me and removed her hand. "You no suffer for me. Is not okay, okay?"

It wasn't in my nature to hand off responsibility so easily. I fixed things when they went wrong. I didn't make them worse.

Adi broke the silence. "You climbed over that big, concrete wall? I would've liked to have seen that."

Sylvia glared at her.

"What?! You have to admit that at their age, that's pretty impressive."

Focusing my attention back on Tia Rosa, I asked her again, "What happened? Why were your prints and hair on the car?"

"I lose balance, okay? My legs shake after wall climb."

"Is because you fat. You need exercise," Abuelita accused.

Ignoring her sister, Tia Rosa continued, "I trip

over feet. I fell on car and police hear me. No time to clean, we run."

Abuelita clapped her hands together. "I have good idea. We do power walk every morning. We bring Lady."

While I was happy to hear Abuelita take an interest in Lady, she clearly didn't understand the situation. "Agent Vasquez told me Tia Rosa is his prime suspect because of the fingerprints and the gray hair on Maria's car. He also suspects that we were the ones to break into José's distillery in an attempt to plant evidence against him."

Sylvia raised her hand to her temples, rubbing them. "Ay, Mamá, what have you done? I told you the next time you get yourself locked up, I'm leaving you in there."

Abuelita had been in jail before? I sensed there was a story there, but it was hardly the time to ask about it.

Turning to me, Sylvia said, "Jessica, I am so sorry. Here your parents arrange for you to have a nice, calm, relaxing trip and you've had nothing but problems since you got here. I can't help but feel responsible for it, and I know these two don't help matters at all," she said, motioning toward her mother and aunt.

"You're very kind, but they're only in trouble because they tried to help me out. Obviously, Agent Vasquez is on the wrong trail, and I think we should help him get on the right one."

Abuelita perked up at that news. "Is about time!"

Tia Rosa clapped her hands. "Is okay! You have plan?"

Before I could respond, Abuelita said, "Right now, no plan. I show pictures and we make cake!"

My nostalgic, carb-loving self thought that was a brilliant plan.

Chapter 14

Abuelita pulled the lid off a tin of shortbread cookies sitting on the counter. Ruffling through the pictures inside, she finally found what she searched for. Holding the picture over her heart, she said, "I gave promise. I keep promise." She held the photograph out.

My breath caught and my eyes blurred. The colors were faded and a crease ran down the middle, separating the two young men in the picture. I knew Dad's twin would look exactly like him, but I still wasn't prepared to see my uncle.

Dad smiled back at me, his arm wrapped around the shoulders of a man who could have been his mirror reflection. Only Dad's long, flowing hair, worn jeans, and woven shirt distinguished him from his brother. My Uncle Eddy. His hair was shorter, but not so short he couldn't style it up and away from his face like he'd been racing a jet or driving a convertible. He wore slacks with creases down the front and a blazer over a pastel t-shirt. He belonged on the set of Miami Vice.

I held the picture up in my trembling hand for Sylvia and Adi to see and braced myself against the solid island.

Abuelita plucked it from my hand, saying, "No faint in kitchen."

My fingers tingled at its loss. "I'm not going to faint," I said, holding my hand out for the picture.

Tia Rosa said, "You keep, Jess. Okay?"

Abuelita leaned in to me, her smile widening as she looked at the picture. Pointing to my father, she said, "Benny was kind, young man. He want save the world."

Sylvia poured coffee. "We all did back then."

"I know that my parents met through Greenpeace, and they often refer to their time here as the best of their lives. It's why they sent me."

"Greenpeace brought more than a few idealistic couples together. Your mom and dad, and James and me. While the trials of life proved too much for my marriage, your parents have thrived on it. I admire them more than you can imagine."

Adi rested her chin on Sylvia's shoulder.

Sylvia kissed Adi on the cheek. "Not that I'm ungrateful. I wouldn't trade my family for anything in the world. I can only imagine how painful it must have been for Benny when Eddy was lost."

I bowed my head under the weight of my memories. "It devastated him. He's never been able to accept it."

"He brave send you here," said Tia Rosa as she shuffled through the contents of the tin.

"Knowing that is what helped me get here. I was tempted to call it quits a few times, but I couldn't do that to him ... or the rest of my family. They were set on me coming."

"Well, I'm glad. Things have been much livelier since your arrival," said Adi.

"You can say that again!" chuckled Sylvia.

Tia Rosa waved a photograph in the air in triumph. "Aha! I know it here! I find it!"

We all leaned forward.

"Oh my goodness, is my mom wearing pearls and shoulder pads in the jungle?" I should have known. My mother never left the house until she looked her best. I guess she'd always been that way.

Adi pointed to the couple standing next to my mom and dad. "Could you wear any more rubber bracelets, Mom?"

Sylvia raised her chin. "I was channeling my inner Madonna. Helen went with the more classic look. We had a lot of fun together."

I couldn't help but notice how she directed the attention away from the handsome man she stood beside and to my mom. He must be the ex. I could definitely see a family resemblance with his firm jawline, muscular build, clear eyes, and height. Jake and Adi had definitely hit the gene jackpot.

Cabs, Cakes, and Corpses

Abuelita picked up the pictures and pinned them on the fridge with fruit-shaped magnets. "These happy photos. Happy time."

The waitress popped into the kitchen, her hands full of orders. I peeked through the swinging door before it shut. A hungry pack of tourists with large hiking packs and dirty boots settled in at the tables.

"Time to get to work ladies," said Sylvia, lowering a stack of white plates onto the counter. She lifted the lid of the pot of chicken and the spices filled the kitchen, making my mouth water. It was that good. I'd have to ask her for the recipe so I could make seco de pollo for my family.

I moved toward the sink where a stack of dishes waited to be washed.

Abuelita stopped me midway. "Jess, you do more important job. You make cake." She pulled ingredients from a cupboard above the extra stove, setting them in the middle of the island. Measuring cups, flower, sugar, nutmeg, powdered sugar, a bar of unsweetened chocolate….

Abuelita patted my hand to get my attention. "Is everything?"

I nodded. She had given me the ingredients for Mammy's goofballs.

"Good. I help Sylvia. You make cake?" She reminded me of a little kid in a candy shop, asking her mother if she can buy a lollipop and anxiously awaiting her reply.

"You kept your promise and I'll keep mine. Thank

you." My eyes teared up again. Instead of pointing her finger at me and saying, "No cry in kitchen," she patted my cheek gently, nodded her head brusquely, and left for the busy side of the kitchen.

The waitresses bustled in and out, their arms full of plates loaded with delicious looking food. Abuelita, Sylvia, and Adi served the meals in an assembly line fashion — Adriana tending to the items on the top of the stove, Sylvia stopping to chop what was needed and stirring the pots nearest her, and Abuelita managing it all with a tasting spoon in hand. Tia Rosa kept the dirty dishes under control.

In a matter of minutes, I had the smooth batter mixed up and ready to fry. I looked over at the gleaming stainless steel double stove, but every burner had a pot on it. Everyone was so busy keeping up with the last of the lunch crowd, I didn't want to interrupt their work. So I took my batter, the sugar, and the chocolate and went over to the extra stove by Tia Rosa. With her help, I found a large container of oil and a pan deep enough to fry in.

Unaccustomed to the gas stove, which had to be lit with a match, I nearly caught Tia Rosa's sleeve on fire when the flame exploded from the burner. I reached up to see if I still had eyelashes. The match burned like a wick all the way to the bottom, leaving a string of charcoal where I'd dropped it.

I overcooked the first goofball, the outside turning a dark brown while the inside was still too gooey. It took some time for the oil to cool to the perfect temperature, but the wait was worth it. I plunked in as many balls of dough as I could comfortably fit in the pan, all the while hearing Julia Childe's voice in my head. "Don't crowd the mushrooms." Thank you for the tip, Julia.

Adi swung through the door. "A customer asked me what we're making back here and if it's for sale."

"I might have to put you on the payroll, Jess," teased Sylvia.

I turned off the burner and put the plate piled with crispy, golden balls on the center table. Once they cooled enough not to burn my fingers, I'd dip them in the chocolate frosting I'd whipped up between batches.

"They beautiful. They taste good?" asked Abuelita, reaching out to take one.

"Not yet. Give me a minute." Taking them off of the napkin soaking up the extra oil, I dipped them in chocolate frosting and arranged them to their best advantage on the plate. Abuelita was right. They were beautiful.

I pushed the plate toward the group gathered around the table. Abuelita lost no time in grabbing the largest goofball and popping the whole thing into her mouth. She closed her eyes, sighed contentedly with her hand over her heart, and chewed slowly.

Adi selected a ball and delicately bit it in half, her eyes narrowing as she tasted it like a food critic.

Before she devoured the rest, she said, "These are fabulous. Like buñuelos, but better."

Sylvia chose the smallest on the plate. "These look delicious, but I don't want to ruin my diet. This little one will do." Popping it into her mouth, she turned her attention back to the stove. It didn't take her long to return for a second. "Life's too short to diet anyway," she justified.

Abuelita agreed, helping herself to the quickly diminishing pile before her. "We add to menu. You teach me?"

"Of course. They are easy to make and take no time at all," I said, content they approved of my sweet-making skills. I couldn't cook a meal to save my life, but I could make desserts. Mammy had made sure of that.

Pleased with my reply, Abuelita grinned and grabbed another goofball, taking it over for Tia Rosa (who was elbow deep in soap suds and dishes) to try.

"Mmm. Is delicious," Tia Rosa exclaimed to Abuelita's applause.

Clearly, the way to their hearts was through their stomachs.

I don't know what it was, but a flood of emotions swirled through me. Maybe I'd had too much sun. Maybe the melancholy I felt when I looked at pictures of my family during happier times had made me sappy. Or perhaps it was the excess sugar I'd consumed. But, as I stood in the center of the kitchen surrounded by friendly chatter and warm smiles, I felt like Anne Shirley when she had met Diana in Lucy Maude Montgomery's classic tale. Only I was so much luckier. Instead of one kindred spirit, I was convinced I had found four.

Chapter 15

I had just made a pot of coffee when someone knocked on the door and entered the apartment.

Abuelita barged over to the small, round dining room table and sat strumming her fingers against the wood. "We need plan. Rosa no go jail."

Adi took the sugar bowl and some spoons over to the table. "Mom sent us up here while business is slow. She's keeping Tia Rosa busy."

Looping my fingers through the handles of two mugs, I joined them at the table with the coffee pot.

"How is Tia Rosa?" I asked.

"She said she's okay, but we don't believe her."

"Rosa say everything okay. She no okay."

Clearly Abuelita was not okay. Her voice carried an extra bite to it and her feet fidgeted to the same rhythm of her fingers on the table.

Adi pushed the sugar to her, and she helped

herself to two spoons full. I put an empty spoon in my coffee and whirled it around.

"Why you do that?" asked Abuelita, looking at me as if I'd hogged all the sugar when I hadn't had any.

"Do what?" I looked at Adi, who also wore a puzzled expression.

"You no use sugar?"

"I like my coffee black. Especially after the sugar binge we just had downstairs."

Adi, who I was learning was the food connoisseur of the family, said, "I can see that. The contrast of bitter and sweet makes an appealing combination."

"But you use spoon? Why use? You stir nothing."

Was it really a big deal? I considered shrugging it off, but Abuelita was in a mood and I didn't want to do anything to make her day any worse than it already was.

"It's a habit, I guess. I like to hook my thumb around it when I drink a hot beverage." I sipped from my mug to demonstrate how "not-big-of-a-deal" it was.

"But you no stir. You no use spoon."

What else could I tell her?

Finally, she said, "You weird."

"Abuelita! The word you want is quirky," said Adi, in my defense.

"No. She weird."

I smiled to reassure Adi. "I'd rather be weird than boring." An odd comment, coming from me — the girl my family conspired against because they thought

I lived in an enclosed, mundane bubble of my own making. They couldn't say I was boring now!

Abuelita patted my hand. "Is okay. I like weird. Is interesting. Now, we save Rosa. How we catch José?"

While I tended to agree with Abuelita, I didn't feel it was in Tia Rosa's best interest for us to ignore other possibilities. "He's not the only one who could have killed Maria. Maybe he has a strong motive, but there were others who had the means to do it."

"He tire of Maria and he want sister. Martha nice and José love children."

Adi shook her head. "That doesn't seem right. There are more peaceful ways to get what he wants. Couldn't he have just asked Maria for a divorce?"

Abuelita crossed her arms defensively. "And if she no agree? He kill her. He guilty. I feel it in gut. He want divorce. She no give him. He kill her. Done!"

"But he needed Maria to drive him around," Adi argued.

"José doesn't drive?" I asked.

"He doesn't. It's not like the US where everyone has a driver's license. Public transportation is so cheap, a lot of people prefer that over the costs of having and maintaining a car."

Abuelita crossed her arms. "José get new ride. No is problem."

I didn't really see the problem either. "Or he was planning to get his driver's license soon." There was that possibility.

Abuelita huffed in her chair, visibly annoyed Adi

and I would cast any doubts on her theory. "Is easy. We have machete. We give to police. Police arrest José." Abuelita smacked her hands together like she was ridding them of dust.

I admired her enthusiasm, but Abuelita's emotions clearly blurred her logic. "It's not so easy. Agent Vasquez will know José's machete was stolen from his parents' property as soon as he goes out there. He already suspects us."

"He suspect Rosa. He estúpido."

"Stupid or not, we cannot hand deliver evidence against us to the police. They'd find my fingerprints on the handle and, with Tia Rosa already under suspicion, it wouldn't take them long to find evidence against you too. Agent Vasquez isn't as stupid as you think he is. Now, while I appreciate that I'd have nice cellmates in jail, I didn't come down here with the intention of spending my vacation in the slammer."

Like a dog with a bone, Abuelita said, "I wash handle. Problem solved."

Did she have to be so stubborn? I tried to empathize with her, I really did, but my patience was wearing thin. Looking to Adi, I asked, "Can you reason with her?"

Adi rolled her eyes. "Welcome to my world. If you can't reason with her, then I don't stand a chance. If Jake were here, I'd ask him to help, but he's not."

That was news to me. "Where is he?"

"One of his guides called in sick, so Jake's filling for him."

"Does he know about the accusation against Tia Rosa?"

She shook her head emphatically. "What good would it do? He'll be away for a week. If we told him, he'd cancel his tour before leaving Tia when she's in trouble, and then she'd feel guilty for making him lose work. Nobody wins."

"Then we'd better solve this before he gets back. Otherwise, you'll have to explain why nobody told him." It was a tough call. If someone in my family was in trouble and I found out they'd kept it from me, I'd be livid.

"We give machete to police. Is easy," Abuelita insisted yet again.

"How do you plan to answer when they ask how you got it?"

"I leave note with machete." Like she left anonymous tips at the police station all the time.

We sat in silence for some time. Could it be as simple as that? Would it work? I had no doubt that Agent Vasquez would suspect us, but so long as there were no prints attached to the machete besides José's, he couldn't prove anything.

"You'll have to pick a time when there are fewer policeman around," I said.

"I go before sun up."

With that resolved, I moved on to the next suspect.

"What about Dario? I think it's too convenient that he was the one who found Maria's body while

José napped inside the house. Do you think he's involved somehow? Could they have worked together?"

Abuelita pinched her lips together in thought. "Is possible he work with José. José make fancy alcohol. Dario sell it."

Adi sat forward on the couch. "You mean, you think he and José might have worked together to kill Maria? While I can see how both men might want to be rid of her, isn't her death bad for business? I mean, there was no other reason for him to be at their house unless they were doing business together."

"True," I said, thinking out loud. "When we were at Martha's yesterday, he made a big deal about telling me that his bar was too good for the puro José makes and sells. However, José did bring back three bottles of brand name liquor. I wonder if he sold them to Dario? On the other hand, if that was José's plan, he wouldn't have offered me a drink on the plane."

Abuelita scoffed. "He know you no drink."

"I drink when I want to. It's just not my habit to accept hard liquor from strangers on airplanes," I said, miffed that she presumed to judge me.

Adi pinched her chin. "I have to admit, I agree with Abuelita. You have 'Good Girl' written all over you."

What? Am I that easy to read? What did it matter anyway? My drinking habits (or lack of) were hardly worth discussing when a murderer was on the loose.

"Let's focus, please. Do you think Dario went over to José and Maria's to buy the bottles?"

"You said there were three of them?" asked Adi.

"Definitely."

"That's more than the allowed limit. Like, a lot more. If José managed to bring three full-sized bottles of imported liquor into the country, he must've paid several people off at the airport. You didn't notice anything, did you?"

"I got through customs before he did. As seriously as they take their job, there's no way he could sneak the bottles through unseen. That explains why Maria was so happy to see the liquor. She jumped up and down in excitement."

"He bad man. He bribe. He kill Maria," Abuelita repeated just in case we had any doubts where her suspicions lay.

"If they could sell them at top dollar to Dario, they could make a pretty penny," Adi commented.

"So, José brings back liquor for Dario in exchange for his help killing Maria? Not exactly a fair transaction if you ask me — especially when Maria was essential to José's business, of which Dario made it a point to say he had nothing to do with. There has to be a better motive." I felt like we were running in circles.

"Remember distillery. Dario no buy puro. He buy adultery liquor."

"Adultery liquor?" I asked in hopes of a translation.

"Adulterated liquor. It's a major problem because importation licenses are hard to get and the taxes are so expensive," said Adi.

"How could Dario sell that without getting caught?"

"First drink good. Second drink good. Third drink not-so-good."

I remembered the inside of José's distillery. The vat of water that smelled of cinnamon and licorice had the same amber color of whiskey. He would have had to add cheap alcohol to the mix or it would just be a glorified, unsanitary tea mixture. "Someone would have gotten sick from that stuff by now. Have you heard any complaints against his drinks?"

Adi set her coffee down. "It happens all the time, but I haven't heard of any specific accusation against Dario. Maybe if we paid a visit to his bar, we could learn something useful."

"If Maria got between Dario and José's lucrative business, that might have given him motive enough to kill her. People kill for money all the time. If we can prove he has tainted alcohol, that establishes a connection and a potential motive. It might be enough."

Abuelita waved her finger in the air. "No good. Dario smart. He no tell secret."

"That could explain why Christian was up in arms yesterday. Dario must be one of his best customers, and if Dario is buying from José, it means

Christian has lost a major source of income," said Adi.

"Was Christian's business legit or do you think he was doing the same thing as José?" I asked.

"I have no idea. Christian comes across as such a slimeball, I wouldn't put it past him to do something illegal."

I chewed on my lip, wishing I had a stick of gum instead. "All we need is one drink. That shouldn't be too difficult."

"Tomorrow Sunday. We go tomorrow. People sad Monday come. They drink."

It was a good idea. I was in no shape to go anywhere sooner anyway.

"Okay, then, we'll go to Dario's bar tomorrow. Would it be worth our while to ask at the hospital if anyone has been treated for methanol poisoning?"

Adi raised her hand. "I'll go to the hospital this afternoon while you nurse your sunburn. The last thing you need is to be outside."

My thoughts exactly. Tomorrow would be bad enough, but today, I was absolutely miserable. "Thank you."

"Okay, so we have José, Dario, and Christian. Anyone else?" asked Adi.

The last one was difficult. I didn't want to suspect them, but their names kept coming up. And they were the ones to potentially benefit the most from Maria's death. "What about Fernanda and Martha?"

I expected to hear objections immediately, but they didn't come.

Abuelita frowned. "Fernanda hide secret. Martha worry."

"And she has every reason to worry. Fernanda wants her mom to marry José. She was more excited at the opportunity Maria's death presented than sad she had lost her aunt. Even if Fernanda didn't do it — which I'm inclined to think she didn't — she could get herself into a lot of trouble unless she's careful. And then there's Martha. José could offer her a stability she hasn't had in a long time." I really hoped it wasn't them.

"Are you still planning on sending Martha food tomorrow?" Adi asked Abuelita.

"I send early. Tomorrow busy day."

Adi picked at her nails. "I think we should try to talk to them when we deliver the food tomorrow."

Abuelita perked up at her suggestion, sitting ramrod straight. "You both go. Fernanda like you," she said to me.

I wouldn't go so far as to say that, but it was worth a shot. At least we had a plan. It was a start.

Chapter 16

My skin was still puffy and red the following morning, but it didn't hurt like it had yesterday. Sleeping had been nearly impossible. Between my sunburn and my brain, which would not turn off, I rolled from one side to the other in an attempt to get comfortable and relax enough to quiet my mind. When the neighbor's rooster started crowing at six in the morning, I finally gave up the struggle and got out of bed. Didn't the singing fowl know the danger of living so near a restaurant?

I took Lady for a stroll around the neighborhood before loading her doggy dish with food. I put it down on the ground and she sniffed at it daintily before looking back up at me with one ear up and one ear down. She cocked her head to the side as if asking what I had put in her dish. Just then, Abuelita came out of the kitchen with a bowl of meaty bones.

Looking down at the dog, I said, "I see how you

are. Why eat dry dog food when Abuelita gives you the good stuff?"

She raised her paw up for me to take and bowed her head with her ears back. It looked so much like an apology, I ruffled her ears and told her, "I can't fault you for having good taste. Enjoy your breakfast."

"Why you talk to dog? She not person. You weird."

Yes, we had established that yesterday. "Good morning to you too, Abuelita."

I followed her into the kitchen and she poured me a large mug of freshly brewed coffee. Holding it just out of my reach, she asked, "What you make today?"

I reached for the liquid ambition, but she pulled it away.

"You're holding my coffee hostage until I agree to bake something? That's low."

She grinned. "I short."

Right behind her, a pile of ingredients were lined up on the center table. The cinnamon was next to the sugar. Mmm, I loved cinnamon and what goes best with coffee than coffee cake — the kind with a crumbly topping that crunches and melts in your mouth.

Holding my hand out again, I said, "Do you have a square baking pan?"

Abuelita handed over my morning caffeine and riffled through a cupboard. She pulled out two baking pans. "One to us. One to Martha," she explained.

"Good idea. Maybe she won't get mad at us for

prying if we offer her something sweet." Going and talking to her had seemed like a better idea the day before than it did at that moment. What if my instincts were wrong and she or Fernanda really had killed Maria?

I measured the ingredients for two coffeecakes, added an extra dash of cinnamon on top of the crumble mixture and popped them in the oven. My grumbling stomach informed me it would be a long thirty minutes until the cake was ready and I could have a square. Ten minutes and another cup of coffee later, Abuelita checked the timer and turned the oven light on to check its progress, then checked the timer again.

Sylvia came into the kitchen from the reception area. "Mmm, it smells so good out in the dining area, the customers are asking what we are baking back here. Is it another one of your creations, Jess?"

"She make coffeecake with no coffee," said Abuelita, once again looking at the timer.

I'd never thought about that. Why was it called coffee cake? There were several desserts people ate with a cup of coffee. Why should this cake be named after its most common accessory rather than an ingredient like its peers? Was it some sort of rebellion? Reining in my deep thoughts, I told Sylvia, "Adi and I are going to take one of them to Martha's with the lunch you send. Maybe she'll know something." I waited for Sylvia to tell me what a bad idea it was for us to go out there, but instead she smiled.

"Agent Vasquez warned you not to interfere with his investigation, but he said nothing about being good neighbors. I think that's a lovely idea. Fernanda asked about you yesterday. I'm sure she could use a friend right now."

For not having made new friends for so long, it sure was easy to do now. I found myself surrounded by real people with real faces instead of virtual friends with avatars in bookish forums and coder chat rooms. It was kind of nice.

Fifteen minutes later, Adi joined us along with Tia Rosa. The coffee cake was a hit, and we cleaned up the pan before the other one could even cool.

Gathered around the island with refilled coffee cups and the crumbs left on our plates, Adi said, "It's too bad you're leaving at the end of the month. I would convince Mom to put you on the payroll in a heartbeat. You could earn good money with your baked goods."

Sylvia said, "You wouldn't have any convincing to do, Adi. If Jess decides to stay, she has a job."

They both looked at me expectantly. I almost choked on my last mouthful of coffeecake. Washing it down with a gulp of coffee, I wiped my chin with the napkin Abuelita handed to me. "I can't stay."

"Why not? You're young and can live anywhere you choose," said Sylvia.

I didn't know what to say, so I laughed. "Then you'd have to put up with me every day, not just for a month."

"They put up with Bertha. You very nicer," said Tia Rosa, garnering approving nods from Sylvia, Adi, and even Abuelita.

My heartbeat pounded in my ears. They were serious. It was ridiculous to make a life-changing decision like that when I'd only been in the country for three days. Goodness gracious, I'd only known them for three days.

What would my family do without me? Dad would fall into a depression, Jessenia would have to hire a sitter to help her with Jayden, Jessamyn would go crazy with her budget, and Mammy would miss me.

Tia Rosa stacked my empty plate on hers. "Change is good. Is okay if you want to stay. You welcome here."

Though the knowledge that I wouldn't have to board a plane to get home was appealing, it was too crazy. Me? Live in Ecuador? Bake for a living? No, it was crazy.

RAIN SLAPPED against the windows and poured down the glass in streams.

Sylvia rushed to plate the influx of orders brought by the tourists seeking refuge from the rain in her restaurant. She handed the plates to Adi, who left a pile of orders on the counter. The sink was full of dishes again. Abuelita occupied herself over the stove.

Being the official taster and seasoner, she had delegated her sister to the role of the dishwasher. Not once had I seen Tia Rosa near the stove. She probably wasn't allowed.

So I put on the green rubber gloves, moved Tia Rosa's footstool out of the way, and set to work. It was the least I could do when they insisted on feeding me lunch every day.

"Jess," Tia Rosa said. "I wash. You dry and put away."

I was about to refuse when she raised a plate. Without the added height of her footstool, she could open the cupboards, but she fell a few inches short of being able to put a dish on top of the stacked plates. It made her climb over Martha's property wall all the more impressive. How had those two managed it?

The breakfast crowd stayed longer than normal, encouraged to remain indoors by the deluge outside. I thought it rained hard in Oregon, but I'd never seen anything like the torrential downpour outside the restaurant. I hoped it would stop before Adi and I had to leave for Martha's.

Sylvia pulled out her plastic containers, loading them with green rice (a delicious combination of rice cooked in blended spinach and garlic) and a dish of pork stew with fried, ripe plantains. She covered the cooled coffee cake with plastic and set it on the top of the food she'd put in a bag for Adi and I to carry. "You'll have to take a taxi. It's still pouring outside. Maybe it'll clear by the time you get there."

From the view out of the window, that didn't seem possible.

We jumped across the river of water streaming down the street, flagging the first taxi we saw. In the few steps it took to get from the sidewalk to the car, my hair dripped and my shirt was soggy. That's Amazon rain for you.

Placing the bag of food between us in the backseat, I finally took in some of the details of the taxicab we had just gotten into. Lo and behold, it was Martin the driver with the duct taped bumper. I had given the cab the benefit of the doubt by thinking that the outside of his car was a poor representation of the inside, but I had been wrong. There was a gash in the seat which he had attempted to cover with a bathroom mat, but the sticky rubber on the bottom of the mat had rubbed off and slid on the seat, leaving little balls of yellow rubber everywhere. I tried to scoot as close to the door as I could, but promptly jumped back into place when my door swung open.

"No problem," said Martin, breaking with no regard to the cars following us to reach over me and pull my door shut. That done, he pounded his fist against the door lock, waving his hand up in the air as if he had just performed a magic trick.

The cars behind us on the narrow one-way street began honking impatiently and Martin put his car in first, grinding gears as he did so and giving Adi and I a major case of whiplash as we bunny hopped into second.

Cabs, Cakes, and Corpses

My neck was already sore and we weren't even halfway there yet. His car smelled nice though. It must have been the red air freshener shaped like a tree dangling from the rearview mirror.

"Is mechanical problem. My car get fixed at shop," he said.

"Hey, you speak English! Fantastic!" I said, seeing an opportunity to ask Martin some questions. I had seen him have quite the fiery exchange with Maria the day I got here.

He smiled. "Is good for business, you know," he said.

"Well, that's smart of you to learn. I imagine the tourists feel better when they can communicate with their driver." I hoped the compliment had the same effect on him as it always did with my sisters. Not that I was a great manipulator or anything, but it usually made them more agreeable to what I was about to propose. In this case, I needed information.

"I remember seeing you at the mechanic the day Maria was murdered. That was an awful day, wasn't it?"

He waved at a man sitting outside in his garden. "It was a terrible day. My car refuse to start and I spent all afternoon at the mechanic." He dropped his voice. "But my day nothing compare to Maria's. Is awful what happen to her."

"Were you friends?" I asked.

"No," he answered immediately. "Definitely not friends. You saw us fight when you arrive, yes? I was angry because she did crooked business with a bar and my friend lost his work. It was not fair."

Adi asked, "Maria took Christian's job? Doesn't he supply liquor to the bars?"

"Yes. He lose big customer two months ago. He about to get the job again, but Maria make promises and Christian, he have no chance." His eyes met mine in the rearview mirror. "I tell Agent Vasquez everything. I was at mechanic all the time and I see who come and who go. I hope he find the killer."

"Me too," I said, looking out the foggy window and processing what Martin had revealed. He had made no accusations, nor had he revealed any suspicions he might have had. In my mind, however, his good friend Christian moved up in my list of suspects. Could he have killed Maria to get his income back? And what about Dario? Martin hadn't said as much, but I suspected Dario was at the center of the conflict between Christian and Maria.

The rain stopped and the sun came out from behind the clouds just as the car in front of us moved. A layer of vapor rose off the wet surface, giving a mystic vibe to the beautiful town. The air felt sticky and heavy.

Adi grumbled, "It's going to be humid this afternoon."

Finally, we made it to Martha's house in one piece. Really, it was more impressive that the car made it in one piece. Adi and I would no doubt have sore necks for a day or so, but that poor car was on its last leg.

Martha was at her gate when we arrived. She left her keys hanging in the door to walk over to us, greeting us with hugs and a kiss on the cheek and insisting on carrying the heavy bag.

We paid Martin and, with a departing wave, he ground into gear. The muffler of his car grated against the gravel as he left. He must've run out of duct tape.

"Come, come," Martha motioned for us to follow her inside. She said something else to Adi, which Adi translated.

"She said she's glad we came. Something has happened."

Martha looked like she was on the verge of tears and she gripped the bag of food to her as if her life depended on it.

Chapter 17

It was noisy inside the house, but no one was in the front room. The chair in front of the gaming center was empty.

"José must not be here," Adi said, voicing my thoughts aloud.

Martha led us into the kitchen and set the bag on the outdated ceramic tiles. Her eyes lit up when she saw my cake.

Adi pointed to me and chattered a mile a minute while I smiled and nodded like a bobble head. Abuelita would have poked me in the arm and told me to stop acting stupid. I really needed to learn some Spanish. I was in the perfect place to do it.

Their conversation culminated with Martha taking my hands and saying slowly, "Gracias." It was thoughtful of her, but it made me feel like a toddler. Yep, I was definitely signing up for a Spanish class.

Martha put the food in the fridge, filled a

Cabs, Cakes, and Corpses

saucepan with water from the tap, and put it on to boil. She pointed to the water and asked me something.

Adi shook her head slightly. "Whatever you do, don't accept," she said with a smile at Martha.

"Is she offering me tea?" I liked tea. It went perfectly with some of my favorite literature.

"She is, but you can't drink tap water. You'll get very sick."

Of course! I had gotten too comfortable at the restaurant. They boiled all their water.

"No, gracias," I said, then had to repeat it when she offered me a piece of the cake we'd brought her.

Adi accepted a tea when Martha insisted.

"Won't that make you sick?" I asked when Martha turned to pull out a box of tea.

"I was born here. I have a strong stomach."

Martha pointed to the large, rectangular table against the wall. She sat facing the kitchen door, which she looked through nervously.

Adi translated as she spoke. Even had I possessed a better vocabulary, I couldn't have understood her low mumble.

"She says: I don't know what to do. I think Fernanda has done something horrible and she won't talk to me. Normally, I wouldn't confide this to a stranger, but I'm a desperate mother. When you came here two days ago, I heard her actually talk to you. And she laughed. I haven't heard her laugh in so long, I'd almost forgotten what it sounded like."

A tear trailed down Martha's cheek and she grabbed a paper napkin from a stack on the table to wipe away the evidence of her troubles, her eyes darting between Adi, me, and the open kitchen door.

"Does she want me to talk to Fernanda?" I asked.

"She says: Yes, please. Fernanda won't say anything to me, but if you could be a friend to her, maybe you can help her where I cannot. I'm so afraid."

"What is she afraid of?" I dreaded that I knew the answer, but I couldn't help anybody if I didn't know what was going on.

Martha wrapped her hands around her steaming cup of tea sitting on the table, rotating it in circles. After a large sigh, she began.

"She says: The day before José returned from Miami, Maria asked if Fernanda would help her prune the trees in their front lawn. She wanted the garden to look nice for him when he got home. Of course, Maria offered to pay Fernanda for her help. So, she took our machete and went to work."

"A machete for yard work?" I asked.

Adi explained, "Most people don't have lawn mowers. She would use a machete to cut branches."

Martha nodded her head and continued.

"She says: Fernanda was a little careless and she left the machete at Maria's. She told me she remembered setting it on the table by the back door in the garage. It's easy to identify because Ana Paola painted bright yellow smiley faces all over it. You can imagine how when I first heard that my sister had been ... Well, the first thing I looked for was my machete. Only, I cannot find it. It's gone. And the police assured me they didn't find it in the garage where Fernanda said she had left it. I fear it was my machete that killed Maria and...." Martha wadded the napkin at her eyes, struggling to keep her composure.

An angry voice from the doorway said, "She thinks I did it." Fernanda crossed her arms and glared at her mom.

Speaking before thinking, I asked, "Well, did you?"

"Of course not. But she's overreacting and is threatening to turn herself in just to keep me out of trouble. Can you imagine what would happen to us if she did that? I'd have to quit school and work to feed my brothers and sisters." Fernanda's eyes clouded up with tears, and she furiously wiped them away.

Martha rose, her arms opened wide to embrace her daughter.

Fernanda stepped out of her way. "Can you believe her? Here she accuses me of murdering my aunt and she wants to hug?" She jabbed at her eyes again, her harsh eyeliner softening around the edges. At that moment, she looked like a scared girl.

It was just a hunch, but I was going with it. "Is that what's really going on? You're upset because your mom thinks you could have done it?"

Fernanda's eyes snapped to me. "Duh!" she eloquently said.

Keeping my voice calm, I said, "I can't even imagine how horrible that must feel and I'm sorry for you."

She looked at me askance and sniffed. "It's the worst."

"What reasons has she given you for her suspicion?"

Her face hardened. "I wasn't sad enough when my aunt died."

I had noticed that too. It's what had made me add Fernanda to my list of suspects.

Martha went over to the counter, bringing a generous portion of cake and a glass of milk. Setting it on the other end of the table, she motioned for Fernanda to sit.

Fernanda, rebellious teen that she was, looked at the cake longingly, but turned her back away to stew some more. It was the same posture Jessamyn had tried to use many times to get what she wanted. I wondered if the tactics I used with my younger sister would be effective with Fernanda. It couldn't hurt.

"It's a coffeecake I made this morning. I might have put too much cinnamon in the topping. Would you mind tasting it to see? Sylvia wants to add it to her menu, but I don't want to poison her customers," I added with what I hoped was an encouraging smile.

She huffed and plunked down in the chair. "If it's to help you out, I guess I can take a bite." She stabbed the corner with her fork and tried hard not to show the least amount of pleasure as she tasted it. Now, I'm not the best baker in the world, but I knew it was good.

"I guess it's okay," she mumbled, taking another bite.

"Thank you for your help. I was worried about it. We worry about the things we care about." I almost gagged at my sappy speech. It sounded like something my mother would say.

Fernanda scoffed disgustedly, "You care that much about cake?"

"Okay, so it was a bad comparison. What I meant to say is that your mom is worried about you. Her emotions have to be so muddled up from this mess, I doubt she sees anything clearly. Come on, she just lost her sister! And from the way she's talked about Maria, she actually liked her! I bet she even misses her."

Fernanda's face filled with doubt. She poked at a crumb on her plate. "I didn't do it," she grumbled.

I believed her. "I don't think you did it either. But I do think you know something you're afraid to say."

Her fork went still and she stared at her plate.

Adi spoke softly to Martha. I guessed she was translating for her.

"I thought all our problems would be solved with my aunt gone. It's an awful thing to think about a relative, but there it is. She was a shrew who bossed my uncle around. He's so good with the kids, I thought he would fit in better here. But just this morning, my mom threw him out of the house. To be honest, I kind of couldn't blame her. All he did was eat and play video games my mom didn't want the little ones to see. Then, he'd disappear without saying anything and expect warm food on the table when he got home. As if my mom hadn't been working her fingers to the bone all day."

"Where did José disappear to?"

"I imagine he was working out at Rio Negro. His parents have a house out there."

Oh, I knew about that. Very well, in fact. I nodded my head as if it was news to me.

"Do you think that's where he is now?"

"Probably. I don't care. He isn't as cool as I thought he was. Unless he's out there, he'll probably show up around lunchtime expecting a meal. It's like having another kid in the house."

I chuckled to lighten the mood. "Typical. I bet Sylvia's food can even rival his own mother's cooking."

"Are you kidding? José's mom is a horrible cook. She makes nothing but rice with a fried egg on top," she said through a smile as close to genuine as her surly mood allowed.

"Serves him right for not being more considerate to your mom." I looked over at Martha and was pleased to see that Fernanda did too. The hint of a smile must have satisfied the craving in Martha's soul. She smiled broadly to her girl and the tears sparkling in her eyes looked to be more of relief than worry.

Chapter 18

"Okay, Dr. Phil, what was that back there?" asked Adi on our way home. After our bone displacing taxi ride, we'd decided it best to walk rather than risk another ride with Martin.

"Seriously? I was flying by the seat of my pants, but there were moments when Fernanda reminded me of my sisters. I did my best to remember all the tricks I used with them." It had been one psychological battle after another until I learned my role as the peacemaker in our family.

"I have no idea what that's like. Brothers, I think, must be different. And Jake has always been protective of me. Promise you won't tell anyone, but he used to play tea party with me. I'd make him a cardboard crown sprinkled with glitter and he'd pretend to drink from the fancy set of teacups Mom gave me."

"Aw, that's sweet! I always wanted to have a brother. Many times, I offered to trade my two sisters for one. But then, I would have missed them so I'm glad it never worked out."

We laughed, ignoring the whistles from the grease monkeys loitering outside the mechanic shop we passed (they must get paid for whistles instead of work), and I thought about Tia Rosa and Abuelita. On the surface, they bickered and fought constantly. But the second one of them was in trouble, they joined forces to protect each other. I liked to think my sisters would do the same for me. I'd had many occasions to bail them out of trouble over the years, but I was the steady, risk-averse one. At least, I was. Until now.

"What are you thinking? It looks interesting from the expression on your face."

I didn't want to bore her with the details on the workings of my perfectly imperfect family. So, I said, "I was just trying to imagine Jake wearing a sparkling crown. And it reminded me of my dad. He's a tall man and he'd fold himself up to sit at my pink, princess table to play with me. I'd make him a peanut butter and jelly sandwich and chamomile tea. He called it a 'world famous' sandwich." When he went through one of his blue moods, I'd take a sandwich to him in bed and he'd try so hard to smile for me.

Adi looped her arm around my shoulders, careful not to scratch my reddened skin. "It's a beautiful memory."

It had been, but it held sadness for me too. There's nothing worse than knowing someone you love is broken and feeling helpless when your efforts to fix them change nothing. The laughter from the park we walked by only deepened my melancholy.

I needed to think about something else. "Thank you for translating for me and Martha. What do you think about what she told us about Fernanda?"

"Fernanda is hiding something, for sure. While her attitude makes her look guilty, she's so open about it, I find it difficult to believe she could be that duplicitous."

"She is hiding something though." I agreed with Adi, but for Tia Rosa's benefit had considered it best to play Devil's advocate.

"Yeah, but it's so obvious. If she had murdered her aunt, I don't think she'd be able to hide it. She has a rebellious streak, but she's not sneaky. Maybe she saw something or is trying to protect someone she suspects?"

"Her mom?" I asked, though I didn't think Martha had anything to do with her sister's death. She was the only person who grieved the loss of Maria.

"No. I can see Martha turning herself in to protect her daughter, but I can't see that she would put all of her kids at risk by doing something so drastic. Especially when we know her feelings toward José."

"Yeah, I feel bad for Fernanda. She really had her heart set on him and her mom making a couple, but even she was able to see how that wouldn't work.

What she said doesn't make me think any worse of José, but it certainly didn't help his cause either. And then there was the mention of Christian losing work to them."

"It sounds like there's bad blood there. I'd like to ask Christian about it, but he's such a slimeball." Adi shivered, her face twisted in disgust. "He thinks he's God's gift to women. If we try to talk to him, he'll assume we're hitting on him."

"And there's Dario. I can't help but think that the tainted alcohol is at the center of everything. It connects him to Maria, José, and Christian. If we prove he sells fake booze, he becomes the strongest suspect. He has money, a business, and a reputation at stake."

"On the other hand, if we prove his drinks are legit, it'll be one less person who could have committed the crime. He'd have nothing to fear."

"Good thing we're going to The Lava Lounge tonight."

Adi nodded. "I'll do anything to clear Tia Rosa and it's as good a place to start as any."

I was already nervous and jittery at the idea of facing Dario on his turf.

We stopped to wait for a break in the traffic to cross the busy street.

Adi jabbed me with her elbow and pointed to a little girl running from car to car at the stoplight, trying to sell candy. "That's something you don't see in the States. You know, it's uncomfortable to have poverty pushed in your face, to see little children who should be at school working on the streets, but what else are they to do if they want to eat? They don't have anyone to help them."

I thought of my nephew, and I was so grateful he had an easier life. He had a father who worked hard to provide a roof over their heads and good food to eat. They had a mother who, while she drove me crazy with all of her art projects and educational posts on Facebook, I had to admire for the interest she took in her growing family. She was an excellent mother. Just like our mom.

Patting my pocket to make sure I had some change, I nodded over toward the little girl. "I have a sudden craving for candy. Let's go see what she has." I pulled out more than enough coin, knowing I would buy whatever it was she had. Even if it was grape flavored. Ew.

With Adi's help, I managed to buy five little boxes of mints — one for Adi, Sylvia, Tia Rosa, Abuelita, and me. When I tried to slip an extra dollar to the young girl, she tried to give it back. I insisted, and she smiled so big, I could see all of her teeth (the ones that weren't missing, that is). She couldn't have been over seven.

Adi said as we walked away, "She'll follow you everywhere you go now."

"Then I'll have to make sure I always have change in my pockets."

Across the street on the corner, I saw someone I

thought I recognized. Seeing as how I didn't know very many people here, I stopped to get a better look. I pointed over to the large electronics store, pulling Adi over so we wouldn't be seen. "Is that José?" I could have sworn it was him, but he was average height and had black hair … just like every other local guy walking down the street. Maybe I was seeing things.

Adi looked all over the place instead of where I pointed.

"At the front of the electronics store. With the saggy pants and backward Yankees baseball cap. Hurry before he goes in!"

"All I can see is his back, but it might be him."

"Do you think Abuelita is right about him?"

"She usually is right about most things, but don't ever tell her I said so."

I held up my little finger. "I pinky swear."

Adi and I looked at each other, nodded as we made a mutual decision, and then promptly crossed the street to stand in front of the large windows displaying televisions, stereo systems, and cell phones. I gasped as I saw the sales prices. "Hot snot, I could buy the same TV for under four hundred dollars back home. Are people really willing to pay this much?" The stickers advertised a sale at two thousand dollars. Talk about a markup.

"They find a way or they spend the next five years making payments. I don't see him, do you?"

I looked between two screens. One displayed a

Cabs, Cakes, and Corpses

soccer game, and another displayed The Terminator. The glow reflecting off the glass of the window made it difficult to see beyond it. "I can't see anything past the screens. Would it be too obvious if we just went inside?"

"And risk being seen by José? I'm sorry, Jess, but with your light and bright red skin, he would most definitely notice us."

She had a point. Then again, if it wasn't him, it wouldn't matter.

A small crowd gathered around us, intently watching the soccer game playing on the large screen. They provided a good cover, so we hung around for a few minutes. The crowd got larger as the team dressed in bright yellow jerseys and black shorts advanced across the field like a swarm of bees. People held their breath and bounced excitedly, their eyes riveted to the screen. The air buzzed with excitement around me, but I kept my eyes firmly focused on the front of the store, hoping José would make an appearance. If it was him, what was he doing?

Shouts and cheers surrounded us and I soon found myself jumping up just to see over the waving arms of the crowd. I got high-fived a couple times. They must have thought I was just as happy as they were that their team had scored a point, made a shot, gotten a touchdown … whatever it was they did in soccer.

Doggedly watching the door, I saw José come out of the shop with a large grin on his face and an even larger box in his arms. Adi saw him too. An employee from the store followed José with two more boxes, following him across the street to flag down a taxi. José laughed and conversed with the employee as they waited, and we saw him tip the guy after his boxes had been carefully placed in the backseat of the car, them being too big for the trunk.

He didn't exactly look like a grieving widower.

We departed from the rambunctious crowd of soccer fans for the restaurant in search of Abuelita. Just maybe she was right about José.

Chapter 19

Baños came alive at night. Sultry salsa, fast-tempo merengue, grinding reggaeton, and classic rock boomed from speakers placed in business entryways to draw in customers. People danced in the street. A man peed in a corner.

I looked away before I saw anything I didn't want to see. Adi said, "We call that a pee corner. Hold your breath as we walk by. It stinks."

Abuelita laughed at me. She, along with Tia Rosa, had insisted on accompanying Adi and I to The Lava Lounge. They had felt a sudden protective instinct to keep us out of trouble (as if Adi and I were the ones to worry about). They wore head-to-toe black and Tia Rosa carried her ever-present plastic bag. I was scared to ask what she hid in it, especially when Abuelita pointed to it and whispered.

"How can people urinate in public like that? Don't the bars have restrooms?"

"We no look. You get used to it," said Tia Rosa.

I didn't think I'd ever get used to that.

Two blocks ahead of us, the street fell into darkness and the music grew louder. Instinctively, I knew that's where we were heading. It seemed appropriate that the scary bar would be in an equally creepy part of town where the street lamps didn't shine. I typically avoided dark bars where the emphasis was on choking on everyone else's cigarette smoke and weaving through a crowd of strangers who had had one too many, so to say I was out of my comfort zone was a gross understatement. Adi looked uncomfortable too.

"You okay?" I asked her when she clutched her stomach. Wow, she was taking this worse than I was.

"Let's get this done," she said resolutely.

Neon lights highlighted The Lava Lounge with a flashing, exploding volcano above it. The music was deafeningly loud and I couldn't help but wonder how we were supposed to learn anything if we couldn't even hear ourselves shout when we stood next to each other.

"Okay, you remember what you're supposed to do?" I yelled.

Tia Rosa shouted, "I watch bottles."

Abuelita said, "I watch Rosa and Adi. I no make trouble."

Adi added, "I'll find someone intent on getting smashed and switch his drink when Tia Rosa gives me the signal. I'm hoping for vodka. Mom makes a delicious chicken dish in a vodka sauce."

"And I'll chat it up with Dario, pretending to be interested in Christian to see what I can find out about both of them. He'll soon tire of me, so I'll poke around to see if he's hiding anything." If I got caught, I'd do the potty dance and ask for the baño.

Taking a deep breath of urine-scented air before entering, I stepped inside with my posse.

It was darker inside the bar that it had been outside. To our right was an open floor where a few talented dancers showed off their skills in the center of the room while others teetered on their feet around the edges, grabbing the walls or holding onto each other when they lost their balance. Strobe lights provided the only lighting outside of a few sparsely placed black lights which lit up my white T-shirt like a beacon. So much for blending in.

In the few seconds it took my eyes to adjust and observe my surroundings, Abuelita took up her post behind a potted fern between the bar and the seating area to the left. Adi, Tia Rosa, and I walked up to the bar.

Dario's teeth glowed as he smiled at us and waved.

"Good evening, ladies," he said in his deep baritone. "Let me welcome you to my humble establishment. I'm honored you've come for a visit," he said addressing me. Pulling out three shot glasses, he selected a clear vodka bottle and poured. "First drink is on the house."

Adi stared into her glass, her fingers shaking as she reached for it. Maybe it was the lighting, but her face looked green. Doubling over, she groaned. "I'll be right back," she shouted, already halfway to the hallway clearly marking the bathrooms.

Dario motioned to Adi's vodka shot. "Maybe Abuelita would like to drink that. I see her trying to hide behind my fern."

Great. Dario was already on to us and Adi was sick. So much for our plans. We'd just have to wing it.

Tia Rosa laughed. "She shy. I take drink to her." I had a bridge to sell Dario if he believed that line.

Some new customers entered the bar and sat, taking Darío to the other end of the counter.

I looked over in time to see Abuelita toss the shot back, downing it in one gulp. I held on to my drink, planning to use it to switch with a tainted one. I would have to take Adi's place — the task I dreaded most. I wasn't very good at meeting new people and nobody sat alone. I'd feel weird joining a group I didn't know. Scanning the drinkers settled at the assorted tables and booths, I hesitated to select a target.

I should have been bolder. Darío came back over to where I sat before I could take my drink and disappear amongst his customers.

"You don't like my liquor?" he asked in an offended tone. I couldn't tell if he was kidding or for real, so I proceeded cautiously while cursing myself for my hesitancy. Lifting the glass to my lips, I took a sip and tried not to make a face as the bitterness of the vodka crossed my tongue and burned going down my throat.

Cabs, Cakes, and Corpses

He must've seen the smoke coming out of my nose because he laughed. "That'll put hair on your chest." As if I wanted hair on my chest. "Come on, down the hatch." He watched me expectantly, not even diverting his gaze when Tia Rosa joined me at the counter.

Mimicking Abuelita, I tossed the rest back and tried not to internally combust. My eyes watered and my throat lit on fire, but I managed to make my cough sound more like a clearing of the throat. It earned me a round of applause from Dario and a group of curious onlookers, one of whom ordered me another round. Great. Just great. Five minutes inside the bar and my grand plan was washed away in vodka.

I raised my newly poured shot up to thank whoever it was who had bought it and Tia Rosa leaned into me. "Change plan. I watch bottles; you talk to Christian." She pointed to someone behind me. Someone who winked at me while squirting his mouth with breath spray.

Tia Rosa patted my leg as she crawled down from her barstool. "Is okay, okay? I tell Bertha new plan. I return soon. You talk nice with Christian." She wiggled her eyebrows, then headed toward the plant where Abuelita still hid.

If she thought I could "talk nice" to a guy, Tia Rosa still had much to learn about me. I flirted about as well as I drove.

"Hey, girl," said Christian, who bore no resemblance to Ryan Gosling (more was the pity), when I turned around. He held his hand out and leaned forward to kiss my cheek, bowling me over with his minty breath and hair gel. "What's your sign?"

Did guys still use that line? I leaned back and shook his hand. One way of greeting was more than enough.

"I've been touched by an angel," he said, raising my entrapped hand to his mouth. I pulled my hand free just before he kissed it, leaving him with puckered lips and nothing to slobber on.

He grinned, smoothing back his long hair. "Ah, you play hard to catch. I like that!"

I breathed a huge sigh of relief. He appeared to be the type of person so assured of his allure, nothing I did or said would discourage him. For my purposes tonight, it felt like a gift in a night of successive failures.

Ignoring his lame pick up lines, I asked, "You're Christian, right?"

"You know my name already? I am flattered." He puffed out his chest. There wasn't much to puff, him being of a tall, lanky build. "What is your name?"

"Jessica."

"You are new in town, yes? I would love to show you around."

"I bet you would."

"I drive a Trans Am."

"Good for you. I understand you're the man to go

to for good, imported liquor." No sense beating around the bush.

"Where did you hear that?" he asked, obviously pleased.

"Dario told me. I met him two days ago at Maria Guzmán's house."

Christian sat down on the empty stool next to me. "That was sad. I had seen her just before it happened. You were there, yes? I had to defend a friend of mine from her attacks. She was not a nice person, but I was still sad to hear she'd been murdered."

Christian's heroic memory of his involvement in the altercation was vastly different than mine.

"You didn't see her after that?" I asked.

He pointed to my drink. "You drank that fast. I didn't even see!"

Sure enough, my shot glass was empty. I looked over at Tia Rosa, who had returned from her consultation with Abuelita. She whistled and looked away.

"What can I say? I love vodka."

"Dario! Pour my friend, Jessie, another!" Christian shouted down the counter.

Tia Rosa sat with her unblinking eyes fixed on the bottles behind the bar. Without taking her focus off her target, she said, "Keep coming the vodka. I help and you act drunk."

Dario set the drink in front of me. "You can hold your liquor."

"No more than most. I can't taste anything after three." I added a giggle for good measure. Hopefully, he'd take my hint and switch to José's mixture for the next one. Then we could beat it out of here before Christian's breath spray burned a hole in my sinuses.

"Three is your max? We'll see about that. Keep them coming, Dario." Christian slipped a fifty over the counter. Gracious, how much did he expect me to drink?

Dario stuffed it in his shirt pocket, saying, "I know what you're doing, and I'm willing to talk later."

Christian turned back to me. "Wow, that was fast."

I looked where he did and saw my empty shot glass. I didn't know how Tia Rosa had managed it, but the drink was gone. Without losing a beat, Dario poured another and stretched over to hand it to Christian.

"You're right. I should slow down." I fiddled with the glass, turning it in circles on the counter and pretending to sip on it. "What did Dario mean? Do you guys do business together?"

Christian zipped the horseshoe pendant back and forth across his gold chain. "I'm the sole proprietor of a successful import business. I specialize in imported alcohol."

"You supply for Dario's bar?" I asked again.

"We're in negotiations. My products are better than his current supplier."

"Who is that?"

"José. He doesn't have access to the best like I do.

It was only a matter of time before he begged to work with me again."

Martin had told the truth. There was a connection between José, Christian, and Dario. Now, all I needed was a sample of the bad liquor to hand off to Agent Vasquez, who could then use it to find the real killer. "Really? I wonder why Dario does business with him if José's products are inferior?" I hiccupped when I saw Dario look our way and made a point of steadying myself against the counter.

A large group of rowdy male tourists, who looked like they had recently graduated from high school and were taking advantage of the country's younger drinking age, entered the bar. Dario was quick to pour their drinks. They appeared to already have had a few.

I tried to pay attention to Christian's reply, but with the added noise, I only caught a few words.

Tia Rosa whacked me on the arm with a force worthy of Abuelita, who had disappeared from behind her plant. "He change. He switch for the boys."

With the eagerness the young men accepted their drinks, they'd be gone in seconds and I had nothing to offer in exchange. My glass was empty thanks to Tia Rosa's enthusiastic assistance.

Time slowed to a crawl as everything happened at once.

Tia Rosa practically fell off her barstool to get to the nearest underage drinker just as Agent Vasquez walked in the front door with a direct view of her. And so he saw her snatch the drink away from the boy and walk to me as quickly as her altered steps allowed. I only needed one guess to know how she'd made my drinks disappear.

Abuelita hustled out from the general direction of the bathroom. "Agent Vasquez here…." she said, her warning dying on her lips as she saw the man glaring at us with his arms crossed.

"Hey, that old lady stole my drink!" the kid complained, to which Tia Rosa giggled.

"He so slow, old lady steal drink," she laughed.

I looped my arm through hers before she fell over and took the shot glass away from her before she spilled it or worse … drank it.

Chapter 20

Unfortunately for the drink-less young man, his friends found his predicament as funny as Tia Rosa did. Christian, no doubt feeling the need to show his heroic side, shoved the boy. And that's how it all started. Fists flew, beer bottles swung, stools broke over heads, shouts drowned out the music, and we were in the middle of it.

I swore I saw Abuelita get a few punches in. Tia Rosa, with the luck of the tipsy, walked harmlessly through the masses and out the door without a knick or a scratch on her body.

Adi came out of the bathroom then, her skin the same green as the Incredible Hulk. I ducked, cradling the drink between both hands to protect it until we could get outside, and made a run for Adi. There was no way we could get through the bar. Pulling her further down the hallway, I barged through a door marked for employees only.

The brightness of the fluorescent lights blinded me and I saw splotches of colored blobs in front of my eyes until I grew accustomed to the light. It smelled like old frying oil.

A worker in a white apron approached me, saying something I did not understand. Bummer. Caught already.

He pointed his finger out the door and spoke in a harsh tone, unhappy we had invaded his kitchen. Looking around quickly, trying to give the impression of being lost, I noticed two refrigerators, a large freezer, and crates of beer stacked along one side of the room. No mysterious boxes or crates with designer bottles.... Oh well. At least I still had the drink hidden in my hands. It would beat all if the cook saw it and took it away when we were so close to freedom.

Adi said something to the cook and he grudgingly showed us out a back door which took us to an alleyway behind the bar. Dario's big, black car blocked one side of the alley, so we ran down the other.

Adrenaline and excitement coursed through my veins as Adi and I made our way down the gravel lane and around the corner.

Agent Vasquez already had Abuelita and Tia Rosa cornered just outside the door of the bar. He was not pleased to see us. I wasn't too pleased to see him at that moment either. If only that made us even.

"I thought I told you to stay away!" he said.

Tia Rosa pushed her horn-rimmed glasses up

from where they had slipped down her nose. "You make me sad, Agent Vasquez. I drown my sad in vodka."

Adi, who had lightened to a paler verdant shade, said saucily, "What, we're not allowed to go out for a drink?"

Abuelita nodded. "I like whiskey."

Agent Vasquez glared at us. "I bet you do. Now, tell me, why are you really here?" He looked directly at me, apparently deciding I was the weakest link.

"We have evidence that José is involved in a bootleg operation." I held up my glass. "And this is our proof." I held it out to him just as the door of the bar swung open. Next thing I knew, the shot glass flew out of my hands, and I watched helplessly as the liquid inside doused the front of Agent Vasquez's polo shirt.

"My proof!" I froze in place, too horrified to move.

"Your proof?" Agent Vasquez flicked the moisture off of his shirt.

"Can you still run tests on it from your shirt?"

He looked at me like I was crazy.

"José has figured out a way to manufacture counterfeit liquor. He sells it to Dario, who then serves it to his customers after they've had enough to dull their taste buds. They're making a killing! Did you know that only this afternoon, we saw José buy a small fortune-worth of electronics from the store? Those things don't come cheap!"

Now looking completely annoyed, Agent Vasquez crossed his arms and appeared to be counting in his head. Knowing it better to remain silent until he had finished, I waited.

Abuelita, however, knew no such restraint. Stepping so close to him, the front of her heels touched the toes of his boots, she jabbed her finger at his chest.

"I learn José to be here tonight. Dario angry because he no show."

"And how much of his fake booze did you drink tonight, Señora Jimenez? You smell like a brewery."

Abuelita ignored him, but when he took a step away from her, she had sense enough to stay put.

"The point is, we have several proofs against José. He likes easy money and, with Maria out of the way, he'd avoid having to split everything with her in a divorce. Or maybe she knew his plans and threatened to expose his secret, thus implying his buyers as well. He comes off like bandit with her dead."

Agent Vasquez looked at me gravely.

I continued, "Wouldn't a man desperate to save his extravagant lifestyle murder his harpy of a wife to ensure her silence? He had a motive and he definitely had the opportunity to kill his wife. You can't really believe that he was enjoying a peaceful nap inside the house when his wife was murdered in the garage."

"What are you talking about?" he had the audacity to ask.

Now it was my turn to feel frustrated. Wasn't it

obvious? "José murdered his wife. Everyone knows he was unhappy with her and he is already involved in another illegal activity."

"That's it? Because he illegally adulterates liquor, he must also be a murderer? Do you honestly think I didn't know about his little side business?"

Abuelita, who now helped Adi hold Tia Rosa upright, waved a hand in the air. "José guilty. You arrest him."

Agent Vasquez balled his hands into fists and set them on his hips. Looking around us and leaning in, he said in a low growl, "I don't care what your suspicions are. You have no clue what's really going on. Because of your interference, I now have to babysit four inept individuals instead of gathering evidence for my investigation."

To me, he said, "I had thought you possessed more sense."

His criticism stung, but had I the chance to live this evening over again, I would still have done the same thing. Tia Rosa was my friend, and it went against my nature to sit idly by while she was accused of a horrible crime.

Turning away from us, Agent Vasquez waved for us to follow him. "Come on. Let me see you safely home."

We all objected in unison.

"I am concerned about the safety of the other residents of Baños with you four on the loose. I will feel better if I see you home."

His giant, black SUV was parked nearby. None of us wanted to sit in the front with Agent Vasquez, so we piled into the backseat and rode to the restaurant like a bunch of felons. Tia Rosa snored.

"Is Sylvia working? I would like to have a word with her," Agent Vasquez said as he parked alongside the square by the restaurant.

"She busy. You talk with Sylvia other day," said Abuelita, looking alarmed.

Tia Rosa snorted. "Sylvia not too busy for talk to handsome man."

"My Sylvia no think he handsome. You drunk."

"She tell me she think he handsome. And I not drunk, okay?"

Agent Vasquez was very quiet in the front seat.

Abuelita flung her door open. "You no drunk? You prove it."

Tia Rosa pulled a Gatorade bottle out of her plastic bag. It was half-full of a clear liquid. "Adi ask for vodka. I save vodka for recipe, okay?"

Adi kissed Tia Rosa on the cheek. "Ay, Tia, thank you."

"Why you act drunk?" asked Abuelita.

Tia Rosa looked up at Agent Vasquez, who now stood towering over her. "I hope escape trouble. But it no work."

Agent Vasquez looked between the two elderly sisters. "Do you even know how to stay out of trouble or does it always follow you?"

Smiling up at him, Tia Rosa said, "Is okay. You good man. I trust you no put me in jail."

His face gave nothing away. Without another word, he crossed the street to the restaurant.

Sylvia stood smiling at the cash register. To her credit, her smile did not fade as we got nearer.

Before Agent Vasquez could voice any of his complaints against us, Sylvia motioned for us to follow her into the kitchen. Pulling five mugs out of the cupboard, she silenced any attempt at speech until she poured the coffee and a glass of mineral water for Adi. It was a smart move. She was the boss in the kitchen. She called the shots. Even Agent Vasquez relaxed his normally stiff pose. You know, he really wasn't a bad looking man. He was obviously a hard worker and possessed more sense than I had given him credit for. He had known about José.

Taking a sip of her coffee and setting her mug down on the middle of the island we had gathered around, Sylvia placed both of her hands palm down on the surface and said, "Okay, you may speak now. What happened?" She looked directly at Agent Vasquez for answers.

He cleared his throat and I got the distinct impression he was nervous. Knowing he had a crack in his armor brought a smile to my face.

Unfortunately for me, Abuelita saw my changed expression. "Why you smile? You estúpida? We in trouble," she grumbled.

Tia Rosa winked at me and nodded.

"These four caused a bar fight at The Lava Lounge," he began.

Raising her arms, Sylvia rushed around the island to alternately pat Adi's and my hair, run her fingers over our faces while her eyes searched for injuries, and generally act very much like a concerned mother between glares at her mother. "Ay, you poor things! How did it happen? You are not hurt, are you?"

Agent Vasquez attempted to interrupt her ministrations, which only earned him a glare stronger than the one she had given her mom.

Adi answered her. "We're fine, Ma."

Turning to address Sylvia, Agent Vasquez continued, "Señora Jimenez—"

"Sylvia," she interrupted. "Do not make me remind you again, Agent Vasquez."

"Very well, Sylvia. I realize that what I am about to ask might be impossible, but I must ask it before anyone is hurt. There is much more to this investigation than meets the eye and I missed out on an important opportunity to discover new information tonight because I had to get these ladies off the premises. Can you please keep them out of my investigation?"

Without hesitation, Sylvia said, "About that. The day Jessica arrived and she accidentally left her stuff in the back of Maria's car, I called Maria to see if she could swing by and drop it off. I mentioned it to my family, but I feel foolish for not thinking of mentioning it to you before. They are such a volatile family, it didn't strike me as odd at the time."

Agent Vasquez pulled out his notepad, ready to write. "What did you hear?"

"There were two men fighting in the background. I had to wait for Maria to go inside so that she could hear me. They were yelling and I heard a sound like they were struggling. Like feet scuffing over gravel."

"Could you identify the voices?" Agent Vasquez asked.

"No, but I took the liberty of calling Martha this evening to ask if she remembered seeing anything. Unfortunately, she and the kids were at the back of the house doing laundry at the wash tank."

Adi added, "Even if she heard something, she probably wouldn't think to look. José and Maria have had the police called on them more than once during their shouting matches."

Abuelita piped up. "Maybe Maria have other man. She dump José. He get angry and he kill her."

Agent Vasquez tucked his notepad back into his pocket. "Until I find out, will you please stay out of my investigation? Do you not realize that your interference only makes you and your sister look guiltier?"

Sylvia plunked her hands on top of her hips. "You cannot honestly believe my sweet Tia Rosa is a murderer. Of all the ridiculous ideas ever expressed in this room, that has got to be the most laughable."

Go, Sylvia!

Agent Vasquez shifted his weight. "I have to investigate everyone and I'm only able to eliminate a suspect when the facts support their innocence."

Sylvia crossed her arms and looked at him incredulously.

Shifting his weight again, he added, "Look, I had hoped my warning would achieve a different result, but I was clearly wrong. Though I do suspect some illegal trespassing and several infractions of transport laws, I do not believe Mrs. Jimenez is guilty of anything other than foolishness. There is a murderer about, and it is my experience that someone who kills once has fewer qualms about killing again. So let me rephrase my warning: If I find any of you interfering in my investigation again, I will lock you up. Is that clearer?"

We all looked at Sylvia. I couldn't speak for the others, but I was waiting for her to toss him out of her kitchen.

"While I appreciate that your threats spring from concern and a need to protect my family and friends, I will ask you to show more respect for your elders and my guest while in my kitchen," Sylvia stared Agent Vasquez down until he bowed his head in compliance. Three cheers for Sylvia!

And then, she turned her attention to us. Pointing her finger in a gesture she must have inherited from Abuelita, she said slowly and clearly, "As for you, it is enough. There is no further need for your involvement now that Agent Vasquez admitted his disbelief in Tia Rosa's guilt. Let him do his job and let's allow Jessica to act like a tourist on vacation rather than feel obliged to tag along with you while you pretend to be detectives. Can you do that? Or is it too much to ask?"

I gaped at her, feeling like my mother was in the room and effectively putting everyone in their place. Even Agent Vasquez looked impressed. Tia Rosa and Adi were the first to acquiesce. Abuelita, on the other hand, widened her stance and returned Sylvia's stare. This would not end well. And it was mostly my fault.

Holding my hands up in a truce, I said, "I've heard there's a lot of cool things to see around here, and it would be a shame not to see them. I wouldn't mind going back to the waterfalls to have a better look. Afterward, I'll make my grandma's doughnuts."

"Doughnuts?" asked Abuelita, licking her lips.

With that one magical word, peace was restored in the kitchen and I went to bed that night with a good conscience, anticipating a glorious morning of sleeping in.

Chapter 21

I rolled over, pulling my pillow on top of my head to drown out the thunder pounding outside and attributing the loudness of the clouds to the high altitude.

Again, the incessant pounding, followed by an impatient voice. "Jessica!"

Cracking one eyelid open, I confirmed it was still dark outside. I didn't believe in waking up early. The early birds could have their worms, and eat them, too, for all I cared.

"Jessica!" Abuelita shouted again, rapping on the door with increased force.

Grumbling to myself, I flung off the covers and trudged to the door. I didn't even bother to put on my nice face. It didn't appear until closer to eight in the morning. Anyone who dared wake me up before my alarm rang deserved to see me grumpy.

Yanking the door open, Lady greeted me with an

extended paw. Her tail thumped between Abuelita and Tia Rosa's legs.

"Some guard dog you are." I shook her paw and struggled to maintain my surly attitude when she nudged her nose under my hand.

Abuelita and Tia Rosa looked much too chipper and alert. My annoyance returned with a vengeance.

"What are you doing here so early?"

Tia Rosa answered, "You want be tourist. We take you to hot spring."

Oh, so they were doing me a favor in getting me out of bed at…. I looked at the clock. "At five thirty in the morning?! I don't enjoy anything at five thirty in the morning. I'll be a tourist after eight."

Abuelita was having none of my whining. Clapping her hands, she said, "You hurry. We go before sun come up."

Looking down at Lady, I said, "Seriously? You couldn't keep these two away and let me sleep? If you're going to stay here, we're going to have to discuss terms and conditions."

"Why you talk to dog? You crazy." Abuelita pushed past me and walked into my room, pulling out the drawers of the dresser to reveal zippers, packets of needles and thread, and notebooks full of Adi's drawings.

"Not as crazy as people who wake me up this early. What are you looking for?"

"Bathe suit." She tugged on the last drawer and

found it bursting with fabric samples. "Where you keep clothes?"

Having brought so little, and knowing I was only staying for a month, I hadn't bothered to rearrange Adi's drawers to situate my stuff. Opening the closet door, I flipped the top of my carry-on open and pulled out a pair of board shorts and a polka dot tankini top.

"We wait. You change. Bring dry clothes."

With that, Abuelita left my room, leaving me little choice but to do as she said. It's not like she'd let me go back to sleep.

In short time, I joined them, carrying my wad of clothes inside a rolled up bath towel.

Tia Rosa held out her plastic bag. "Put dry clothes here. I carry."

Resigned, but still not happy about it, I asked, "Where are you taking me?"

"Las Piscinas de la Virgen is hot spring under waterfall. Is close. We walk." Abuelita turned for the door, holding it open for us.

"Baños have many waterfall. Is why it have name, Baños de Agua Santa," explained Tia Rosa.

"Holy Toilet Water? That's sacrilegious."

Abuelita poked me with her finger. "You need learn Spanish. Baños no mean bathroom only. It mean bath. Holy Bath Water."

I still thought it was an unfortunate name for an otherwise charming town, but I had woken up enough to know to keep my opinion to myself.

Lady clambered down the steps ahead of us, grabbed a meaty bone from her food dish, and returned to her post in front of the door. Traitor. Abuelita had clearly bought her loyalty.

The pre-sunrise air had a chill to it. The bakeries hadn't opened for the day yet, but the breeze was heavy with the comforting smell of fresh baked bread. Birds chirped and whistled, rustling the leaves in the trees as they hopped around the branches and sang. It was hard to stay in a foul mood when such pleasant smells and sounds invaded my senses.

"The mineral water good for heal skin," Tia Rosa said three blocks later.

I raised my arm. The blisters were drying up, but I was now peeling much like a snake shedding its skin. It looked as glamorous as the comparison sounded.

Deprived of at least two hours of slumber and my morning cup of coffee, I didn't bother to make conversation. Nothing I said would make much sense anyway. Still, I didn't want to be rude, so I nodded in acknowledgment and tried to smile at Tia Rosa as she explained the healing properties of the mineral springs.

Ten minutes later, we stood at the foot of a waterfall running over the side of the mountain and lit by green lights at its base.

There were several pools and few enough people, I didn't mind stripping down to my swimming suit and dipping a toe in the water of a small pool nobody occupied near the waterfall. I soon understood why the other pools were more popular. The water was scalding. Just how I liked it. Sitting along the edge, I slowly lowered myself into the murky water, reminding myself that the color had everything to do with minerals and nothing to do with dirt. My muscles knew it. They melted into soft putty within seconds.

Sighing because breathing took too much energy, I let the warmth envelop me like a blanket Mom or Dad used to snatch from the dryer and wrap around me when I was cold or sick.

"Open eyes. You miss sun," snapped Abuelita.

Sure enough, the sun was on the rise. A minute ago, it had been completely dark outside and now, bright yellow rays illuminated the clear sky and sparkled off the steam rising from the pools. I looked at the waterfall behind me and appreciated the uniqueness of the place I was at. Where else could I relax in a natural, hot water spring at the base of a mountain surrounded by cascades? No wonder Mom and Dad had loved it here.

Tia Rosa bumped into me. Her glasses had fogged up so that she groped around blindly. "I sorry. I no see with glasses. I no see worse with no glasses. You see waterfall? I paint it at art class with Miss Patty. She great teacher."

"I'd like to see it."

"You come my house and I show it you. I make delicious lunch."

Cabs, Cakes, and Corpses

Abuelita scoffed. "How you make delicious lunch? You no cook."

Tia Rosa's face crumpled up. "I make best sandwich with tuna fish in Baños. Is world famous!" Her plump cheeks dimpled in pride at her accomplishment.

Rolling her eyes, Abuelita said, "You open can. You great cook."

Coming to Tia Rosa's defense, I said, "I can bake, but I'm a horrible cook."

"You put two cup salt in cookie? You put sugar in smashed potato?" countered Abuelita.

"Is no fair. That before I get glasses. Sugar and salt look same."

Abuelita shook her head. "She confuse vinegar and olive oil. My kitchen stink for week."

"The bottle look same," Tia Rosa huffed.

As poor a cook as I claimed to be, I had to admit that not even I would confuse vinegar for oil. More than her eyesight was at fault there. Salt for sugar, on the other hand ... I was glad to know I wasn't the only one to make salt licks instead of cookies.

"Like spray for stinky bathroom?" Abuelita harrumphed. "She use Glade to clean dust for two month and she no smell it."

I bit my lip to hold in my chuckle.

Tia Rosa didn't seem to mind. "My house smell like many lemons, okay?"

"It stink like you make kitchen stink."

Tia Rosa had finally had enough. "Is not your

kitchen. Is Sylvia's. You bossy woman and you think you great cook, but Sylvia best."

"No is true. Adi is best—"

"She no want to cook. She make the beautiful dress, but you no like. Why you no help her?" Tia Rosa didn't back down when Abuelita got in her face.

"Adi need stable work. The dresses is dream."

"She is young. If you good abuelita, you support her dream. You let her try." Tia Rosa shoved her slipping glasses to their perch on her button nose.

"If you so good tia, you make studio for Adi. She no have room for to work in small apartment." Abuelita stepped forward, but Tia Rosa didn't budge.

"If you no do it, I do it. She good girl and she work hard."

"You let her fail. You terrible tia."

"Why she fail? Jake make good business. Sylvia make good business. They help her." Tia Rosa looked at me and I tried to duck under the water before she dragged me into her argument. But I just couldn't bring myself to dunk my head in the brown pool. "Jess help. She good on the computer."

"No. Today, Jess teach me fry the balls."

"They're called goofballs," I corrected, not too keen on becoming known as a fryer of balls.

"How Jess help Adi? She no speak Spanish." Abuelita looked so smug, I spoke before understanding the meaning of her words fully.

"I'm signing up for classes at the language school next door." Take that, Abuelita!

Tia Rosa beamed at me in pride. (It could have been that her face was flushed from the volcano-heated water, but I liked the other option better.) "Hugo and Esmeralda wonderful teachers. You speak Spanish very fast and we make studio with Adi. You do the thing with computer. Is good plan!"

She looked so happy, I couldn't spoil her plans until I could think of how to do it gently. What she planned would take much longer than one little month and I had no intention of staying any longer than the return date on my airplane ticket.

Abuelita pinched her pointy chin between her fingers. "I hate admit it, but you right. Baños no have good cake. Jess need stay more time. If Adi have studio, Jess have bake shop. Is good idea."

Suddenly, the hot water felt nauseating. I hopped up to sit on the ledge, leaving my feet to dangle in the pool while my body steamed in the cooler air. If I didn't interfere soon, my troublesome friends would make plans for me and get their hopes up.

"First things first, I need to learn Spanish. Remember, I'm only here for a month."

They unanimously waved off my reminder like they didn't believe me.

"Seriously, I'm only here for a month and I know I can't learn enough Spanish to run a business. I can, however, teach Abuelita and Sylvia some of my recipes. I'd love to do that."

Again came the disbelieving, dismissive waves as they chattered between themselves in the language they knew I didn't understand. The stinkers. If I left them to their own devices, I'd soon be running a doughnut shop in a foreign country. It was crazy.

They clearly had a plan to which I was central. Hustling me into the cooler pool, and then into the changing rooms, they marched me back across town just as the English school above the ice cream shop was opening for classes. They enrolled me in an advanced class which guaranteed some level of fluency within a month, provided sufficient practice. We left there with my hands full of brochures and printouts of homework I needed to complete before my first class that evening.

My head was still in a whirl, and my hair was still wet, when we returned to the restaurant and what I hoped was a hearty breakfast. Too much thinking and not enough caffeine and nourishment had turned out to be a terrible combination for my future, which Tia Rosa excitedly shared with Sylvia and Adi the second we set foot in the kitchen.

Ignoring her, Sylvia smiled sympathetically at me and pushed the basket of croissants in my direction while Adi poured a cup of coffee and set it below my nose.

"Fernanda called for you a few minutes ago," Adi said. "She sounded frantic, but she wouldn't tell me what was going on."

"Why don't you call her while I stir up some scrambled eggs and ham?" suggested Sylvia, motioning to the phone on the wall above the coffee maker. "Her number is under Gustamante in the address book. It sounds like she's home from school, so she'll probably answer."

I punched in the numbers and Fernanda answered on the first ring.

"Oh, good, it's you. I don't know what to do. My uncle José went missing last night and it's all my fault." Fernanda's voice trembled as the words tumbled out of her.

"Slow down, Fernanda. What happened?"

I heard her sniff and knew she was crying. Finally, in a whisper, she said, "I killed Uncle José."

Chapter 22

"What?" I asked more in astonishment than in a desire for her to repeat her confession.

"Well, I didn't actually kill him, but I might as well have done it. He's gone and we don't know where he is."

"Why do you say you killed José then?"

The kitchen fell silent and the ladies gathered around me to listen, their hands over their mouths in various stages of shock.

"I said I didn't see who he fought with the day my aunt Maria was murdered, but it was a lie. I did see. I just didn't want to believe that he was a … criminal." She said the word in a whisper, like she still didn't want to voice the accusation aloud.

It had to be about a boy. A boy she liked. She didn't have to tell me, but I encouraged her to, knowing it'd be a huge weight off her shoulders to unburden herself from the secret she suspected had not only brought her aunt to her early end, but had led to the disappearance of her uncle.

Abuelita harrumphed. "I still think José kill wife."

If he had fled, I was inclined to agree with her. "Who was it that argued with him and do you think this person murdered your aunt?"

"It was Christian," she said after a very long pause.

"And do you think Christian killed your aunt?"

Eyes widened and gasps were stifled. Except for Abuelita. She looked annoyed. "Christian no do it. José kill wife. I feel in my gut," she insisted stubbornly.

I had been so convinced of the same just a few moments before, but as the pieces fell into place, a new suspect came to the front. A man who desperately wanted to improve his situation, who liked to flaunt his cash and so would need to have plenty on supply. A man who we now knew had fought with José the day Maria was found murdered in her car.

Fernanda said, "I don't want to think Christian capable of doing it, but she did take away one of his best contracts because she offered a much lower price to Dario. Christian was not happy about it at all. He was afraid he'd lose more business to her."

Yikes! He definitely had a motive. "Why do you think he might have killed your uncle? How do you know José isn't alive?"

"Well, I don't know for sure, but Uncle José didn't show up at lunch or dinnertime yesterday. And we got a call from Dario this morning asking where he was.

Evidently, my uncle was supposed to bring a batch of liquor to him and he never showed up."

Not good. Not good at all. Abuelita had overheard the same at the bar the night before. José never showed. But was it because he ran away? Or because he was dead?

"Fernanda, you need to tell all of this to Agent Vasquez. It could help him solve this case."

"No! What if he puts me in jail for lying?"

"You're a minor. He wouldn't do that." Not that I knew so for a certainty. "Tell him that you just remembered. That you didn't know it might be important or something. If you don't do it, I will."

"Oh, good! Thank you so much for talking to him for me. I knew I could trust you. You're the best friend ever. Gotta go! My baby sister is crying. Bye!" The receiver clicked.

I stared at the phone, feeling like a manipulated bonehead for falling into her trap so easily when I knew better.

Sylvia rummaged through a pile of cards inside her address book and handed me Agent Vasquez's card. "We heard," was all she said.

Okay, so they all knew how stupid I was, but at least I wouldn't have to repeat the entire conversation. This was just not my day. I stabbed the numbers with my finger, and was pleased when Agent Vasquez's phone went straight to voice mail. I asked him to call me at his earliest convenience and left it at that.

Cabs, Cakes, and Corpses

The waitress came into the kitchen, ready for more orders. None were ready.

Clapping her hands together, Abuelita said, "Enough talk. Back to work."

She stirred the contents on the stove, checked the seasoning, and barked orders. Adi, who looked like she felt much better today than she had last night, lowered a stack of plates, and Sylvia cut fruit while occasionally stirring the ham and eggs on the stove top. Adi spooned out the orders, comparing them to the papers on the counter. In a matter of minutes, they had fallen into an easy rhythm and the stack of customer orders on the counter diminished.

As was becoming my custom, I joined Tia Rosa at the sink and set to work on the dishes. Who was it that said they did their best plotting while doing the dishes? Probably a mystery writer. After the events of the last few days, I was determined to brush up on my Agatha Christie novels. Not that I expected any more murders during my stay, but after being so convinced José had murdered his wife, I felt completely inept when it now became equally clear that the villain all along had been Christian. The more I thought about it, the more obvious it was. That's probably why Agent Vasquez hadn't answered his phone. He was too busy arresting Christian.

As the day passed without any return calls from Agent Vasquez, my certainty grew. Nobody talked about the murder, José's disappearance, or Christian's involvement. It became the elephant in the room that everyone thought about, but no one wanted to mention. I didn't want to lock horns with Abuelita. She was still convinced José had done it. And maybe he had. What did I know?

It was about an hour before dinner time and the dining room was empty. As promised, I had mixed up a batch of doughnuts during the afternoon. They hadn't turned out as airy as I liked, but the sugar icing I dipped them in more than made up for their density. I separated some of them to dip in chocolate, but I'd run out of cocoa powder. I'd run to the store later while they cooled.

Chasing our binge of sugar with bitter coffee out in the dining room, we were surprised when a giant floral arrangement carried by a minuscule person came through the door. There must have been at least two dozen red roses arranged in the form of a heart, accented with poofs of Baby's Breath and surrounded by large green leaves with red veins.

We circled around the reception counter, where the delivery person set the flowers. To be honest, I thought it was a bit tacky, but then again I had always been a wildflower kind of girl. Like Marianne Dashwood. Still, roses were roses and the flowers were beautiful even though they couldn't help being arranged into a heart.

Abuelita plucked the card off of the plastic tongs holding it. Opening the gold envelope and reading the note's contents silently, she clutched her stomach and started laughing. Tia Rosa leaned over and soon joined in her merriment.

Finally, Abuelita controlled herself enough to extend the card to me.

Not appreciating her joke, I folded my arms. "Those aren't for me. I've only been here for four days and look like a roasted tomato with leprosy."

Abuelita pushed the card at me insistently.

I plucked the card from her hands, glancing down at the note before passing it on to its rightful owner (Adi, duh!) when I saw my name on the card. My face burned in embarrassment, and I knew my cheeks were just as red as the roses in the arrangement.

They ganged up on me, clapping and squealing excitedly.

"What does it say? Read it out loud!" said Adi.

My mortification was complete anyway. I had nothing else to lose.

Holding up the card and clearing my throat, I read loud enough to avoid having to read it again,

> "Roses are red,
> your eyes are blue.
> Sugar is sweet,
> but not as sweet as you."

SYLVIA LAUGHED. "Your admirer doesn't win any points for originality. Does it say who it's from?"

I looked at the paper, but there was nothing else there.

Looking a little worried, Adi said, "It could be from Christian. It's something he'd do."

I wished the floor would open up and swallow me. I knew my embarrassed reaction was anything but normal, but it was as awkward as heck to have a murderer be the first man ever to give me roses.

Adi draped her arm around my shoulder. "Welcome to Ecuador, love! This'll probably be the first of many to come during your stay here. It is impressive, though. You haven't even been here a week."

Abuelita shrugged her shoulders. "What you expect? She pretty and she shaped like woman." She formed a circle with her hands, as if I didn't know that my figure tended toward the round.

Adi stuck her tongue out at Abuelita. "You're just mad that I'm her best friend instead of you," she said sticking her nose up in the air and speaking haughtily.

I was truly speechless. Flowers from a murderer. Abuelita's favorable description of a body I always felt could stand to lose fifteen pounds. Adi's claim of me as her best friend. Nobody ever fought over my friendship. I wasn't cool or interesting enough to fight over. I wouldn't let their praise go to my head, but maybe I wasn't as bad as I thought. For years my family had told me the same, but they were my family and they were supposed to say things like that.

The bell above the door rang, and I saw Agent Vasquez. He looked like he had had a rough day.

Sylvia met him halfway across the room. "You hungry?" she asked. Abuelita and Tia Rosa stepped in front of me. As if they could hide me or offer any kind of protection. It was a sweet gesture.

"I'm famished," he said, taking a seat at the table nearest us.

Slipping past my elderly defenders and sliding into the chair opposite Agent Vasquez, I asked, "Have you arrested Christian yet?" I had got past them, but they stood behind me.

He sighed, his shoulders slumping from their normal stiff posture. "And why should I do that?" he asked.

"He is … I mean, was … José's competition. And they were seen fighting the day of Maria's murder. I called to tell you about it earlier, but your phone went to voice-mail."

He looked at me, his sigh full of long-suffering. "I do wish you would stay out of this. It keeps getting worse and worse."

"Did you find José?" I asked.

"How did you know he was missing?" he asked, completely exasperated.

"Fernanda called me. She was worried and needed to talk."

Abuelita added, "Jessica no look for trouble. Is true. Fernanda call."

He ran his hand through his short hair, massaging

his temples and resting his thick hands at the back of his neck. "Yeah, she had reason to be concerned. I just got back from his parents' property at Rio Negro. José was found out in the middle of a sugarcane field."

"Found?" I was glad I was sitting down.

Agent Vasquez nodded. "He was murdered."

Chapter 23

"Murdered?" Sylvia asked from the swinging door. She plunked a fried trout over a bed of rice and a side of boiled potatoes with peanut sauce in front of Agent Vasquez, who took a large bite before answering any questions.

"How was he murdered?" Adi asked, following Sylvia in from the kitchen with an offering of two of my glazed doughnuts. Agent Vasquez looked longingly at the doughnuts as he dug into the food on his plate. Real food first. Dessert later. Not at all the philosophy Mammy had instilled in me. If you ate all the food on your plate, you ran the risk of running out of room for dessert. Better to eat dessert first, and then you avoid overeating dinner. Judging from Abuelita and Tia Rosa's habits, I'd say they had long ago accepted Mammy's reasoning. Sensible ladies.

I chattered in my own head, grateful to Agent Vasquez for being hungrier than he was anxious to share the gruesome details of José's murder. I'll admit to being curious, but I was also terrified. Two murders within four days. And both of them people I'd known — if only briefly. Poor Fernanda. She would take this harder than anyone. She'd forget her uncle's faults, as death had a tendency to do, and his absence would weigh heavier on her for it since she was the one to withhold evidence to protect a dude she had a crush on. For her sake, I hoped Christian was innocent, but José's murder pretty much confirmed his guilt.

Gulping down his glass of pineapple juice, Agent Vasquez finally spoke. "José was murdered the same way Maria was. I'd bet it was done by the same person with the same weapon."

"A machete?" I asked.

He nodded. "Oh, by the way, thank you for dropping off the anonymous note and stolen machete. I put it back in his shed for his parents to use. They've been advised not to continue his bootleg operation, but they can still make puro and will be grateful to have it back."

I didn't say, 'You're welcome' at the risk of incriminating myself. Instead, I asked, "How are his parents?"

"They're tough people. I suspect they'll be fine sooner than most. Their house was already full of concerned neighbors when I left. No doubt, they'll eat better this month than they have all year. Some of the younger men offered to help them cut their fields and work the press until they can handle things on their own."

"That's really nice." I was ashamed to admit to myself that I didn't even know the names of my neighbors in Portland. (Except for the baristas at my favorite coffee shop, but they wore name tags so that hardly counted.) And if I showed up on their doorstep with a casserole dish, I'd get strange looks and quite possibly a restraining order for my trouble. Ah, city life.

Agent Vasquez inhaled the rest of the food on his plate while we sat around him in contemplative silence. Abuelita was still in denial and most likely trying to figure out how José still could have done it. God forbid her gut feeling be wrong.

"I haven't had a decent doughnut in years," said Agent Vasquez as he pulled the dessert plate closer to him.

"Well, these aren't as light as I like them, but they still taste good." The humidity had made my dough sticky and difficult to work with, but I was determined to give it another go until they came out perfectly.

He consumed half a doughnut in one bite. I sighed in relief when he closed his eyes and chewed slowly.

"These are finger licking good, Miss James. Do you make any other flavors?"

Through my grin, I asked, "What's your favorite? I need to go to the store to grab a few things for the icing anyway."

Agent Vasquez's face lit up with delight and he said with feeling, "Chocolate."

Everyone except Abuelita laughed. She clamped her fingers around Agent Vasquez's forearm when he reached for his second doughnut. "If Jess give you chocolate, what you do for her?"

"Mama!" complained Sylvia.

Agent Vasquez chuckled. "No, Sylvia, I can appreciate what your mom is up to. She sees an opportunity and she's smart enough to take advantage of it."

Looking between me, Abuelita, and Tia Rosa, he said, "In exchange for two chocolate frosted doughnuts, I will not make you wait for my report to find out the conclusions my men and I have drawn about Tia Rosa's involvement in Señora Guzmán's murder."

Without a second thought, I extended my hand to him. "Deal!" Surely, his calling her "Tia Rosa" instead of his normal Señora Jimenez was a good sign.

Much like the man himself, his handshake was firm and resolute.

He looked at Tia Rosa. "Though your own actions put you on my list of suspects, you have an airtight alibi for the night of José's murder. I can attest to your presence at The Lava Lounge during the time given by the coroner for José's death and, while there was evidence of your presence at the scene of his wife's murder, the evidence itself is non-conclusive."

Abuelita jumped up from her chair, closely followed by Tia Rosa. They clapped and exclaimed around the table where they hugged Agent Vasquez multiple times, nearly knocking him over in their enthusiasm. I considered joining them, but he had his arms full as it was. I would, however, make good on my promise. I was so happy, I'd give him a half dozen chocolate doughnuts.

"I'll run to the store really quick," I said as a group of hungry diners entered the restaurant from the darkness outside.

Adi stood. "Do you want me to go with you?"

I considered. The grocery store was only three blocks away. The chances of me running into Christian were pretty slim. I could wear my black hoodie and would come and go unnoticed in the streets. "No, thanks. I can be back in ten minutes tops and Sylvia needs your help here."

Abuelita and Tia Rosa got up to join me, but Agent Vasquez placed a hand on their shoulders. "I have some questions to ask you. I ran a criminal history check on you and some interesting things popped up."

Tia Rosa looked up at him with an impish grin on her face. Abuelita grumbled and sat back down.

To me, Agent Vasquez said, "If you don't come back in a timely manner, I'm coming after you. I don't think you're in any danger, but just to be safe, don't stop to talk with anyone and return as quickly as you can."

As much as I wished to listen in on their conversation, I had frosting to make.

Patting Lady on my way up to the apartment, I grabbed my lightweight, black sweatshirt and walked as fast as I could to the grocery store, weaving through the tourists strolling through the streets looking through restaurant windows for a place to eat.

A honk made me look over. Martin waved. "You need a taxi?" he asked.

"No thanks, Martin. I'm not going far."

"Tomorrow, you should let me drive you up to Luna Runtun. It has a great view of Baños."

"We'll see." I wasn't about to subject my aching neck to that kind of torture anytime soon. "I wouldn't want to take you out of your way."

He laughed. "I am a taxi driver! Is what I do. Besides, my house is on the way." A car behind him honked.

With a departing wave, he said, "See you tomorrow."

Not if I could help it, although it was nice of him to offer.

The market where fresh fruits and vegetables were sold was closing its doors for the night. I glanced at my cell phone for the time. Seven o'clock. There must be a soccer game or something on. At least, the grocery store was still open. I'd have to hurry back if I wanted to frost the doughnuts and make it on time to my first Spanish class.

Peeking down the aisles, I found the section I was

looking for. The assortment of chocolate wasn't as diverse as I had hoped, but what they had was good quality. Selecting a bag of cocoa powder and grabbing another powdered sugar for good measure, I spun around with my treasures in my hands and rammed into a shopper who reeked of mint.

My heartbeat raced in my chest and I turned around to run away from Christian.

Chapter 24

"Wait, Jessie! You like the flowers, yes?" he asked, but I was already halfway down the aisle on my way out of the store.

I heard his shoes squeak against the waxed tiles behind me. Sweet crud, he was following me.

"I want to talk to you," he said.

No way, José. Oh God, José! His killer had sent me flowers and was chasing me in the grocery store.

By now I was at the front of the store with Christian hot on my trail. I couldn't hear what he or anyone else said over the sound of my heartbeat pounding in my ears. Running out of the store and into the street, a city bus went by. I considered hopping on it, but Christian could've seen me through the windows.

I heard him call my name from behind me. I needed to hide. Quickly. The metal doors closed the market. I couldn't lose him in there. But parked on the other side of the market, I saw a pickup with a black tarp covering its bed.

Darting across the street just before the bus could take off with its passengers, I made a mad dash for the back of the pickup. Crouching behind it, I saw Christian cross the street in my direction. Darn.

On the street corner, my little candy-selling friend walked toward me. I waved her away, putting my finger in front of my lips and pointing in Christian's direction. His back was to me now. The little girl engaged him in conversation, but neither of them moved away. If he turned around, he'd see me.

Not seeing any other option, I pulled up the tarp and crawled into the bed of the pickup as quietly as I could manage, slowly covering myself with the plastic and hoping the sound of passing vehicles would muffle the noise I made.

I heard feet scuffing directly behind the pickup and held my breath just in case Christian could hear me. The pickup shook and vibrated as someone turned on the ignition. Oh no. I chanced a peek out of the corner of the tarp. Christian was standing an arm's length away from me. If I got out now, I'd practically fall into his arms.

Panic carried me away for about two blocks before I calmed myself enough to think clearly. Okay, what were my options? Ew, what was that smell? My stomach wretched at the nasty odor accompanying me, and the perverse need to see what the source of the stench was almost overpowered my need to focus. Focus, Jess, focus on the problem.

Baños was a small town plentiful in one way streets and traffic lights. Surely, the pickup would have to stop eventually. I'd just wait until it stopped and scramble out. No problem. I moved into a more comfortable position with which to exit the back of the pickup at its next stop. My knees ground against the metal grooves, and soon my feet fell asleep. We hadn't stopped yet.

I peeked out of the tarp again and saw that we were no longer downtown, but I could still see the lights of town.

Duh! My cell phone! Pulling out phone, I dialed the restaurant. They'd be wondering where I was. Agent Vasquez would be at the grocery store asking about me by now.

I started talking as soon as someone picked up, hoping my cell phone signal would hold long enough to get help. "I ran into Christian at the grocery store. I totally panicked, might have overreacted a bit, and now I'm in the back of a pickup heading to Lord knows where."

Silence.

"Hello?" I asked, checking my signal strength on the screen.

The speech started out garbled, but it cleared enough for me to hear Sylvia's voice. "Describe the pickup to me. Describe everything you see around you."

Cabs, Cakes, and Corpses

"It's a white and green pickup with a black tarp covering the back. It said something about Luna and tuna on the side." Like the name of that place Martin had mentioned. It sounded ridiculous even to me, but I hoped my friends would have more sense than I did. I wasn't feeling too smart kneeling down in the back of the pickup driving to some unknown destination with something disgustingly smelly behind me.

"That's a pickup taxi. Was it parked in front of the market?"

Hope surged within me, soon to be dashed as my phone beeped at me and the call cut. Yanking the phone away from my ear, I looked at the screen again, tapping it in disbelief. Dead battery.

"It figures," I complained aloud, shoving my lifeless phone back into my pocket.

I felt the weight shift in the pickup as we drove down a hill and a crate rolled toward me. Something scratched against my leg. To my horror, it was a crate full of dead, plucked chickens with their feet poking out of the sides and their heads flapping over the edge. I had to open the tarp before I tossed my cookies in the back of the pickup.

The top of the tarp lit up as we went by some kind of a light. I pulled it back enough to avoid gagging and saw dozens of dead, plucked chickens in the stacked crates behind me. I squealed as something wet pooled around my bare knees and toes. Why had I worn sandals?

The crates and chicken goo slid back as we went

up an incline. We drove for quite a distance. I would've guessed it to be at least a half an hour, when in reality, it was probably closer to ten minutes. Being a stowaway and kneeling in squalor had a way of making the time crawl.

Finally, the pickup stopped. Pulling back the tarp, I climbed out, trying to go unnoticed but having a hard time walking on numb feet. How on earth would I be able to explain what had happened?

The pickup had parked in front of a small house off of a main roadway that wasn't used enough to be paved. It was dark and I was in the middle of nowhere. I couldn't see any other lights anywhere around, but knew that if I went downhill, I would eventually get out to the main highway and to help.

It would be a long walk in my flip-flops.

A man's voice called out behind me. I had not escaped detection after all. He pointed to me and he pointed to the back of his pickup. While his voice didn't sound angry, he certainly sounded puzzled.

Doing the best I could with my limited Spanish, I said, "Gracias. Um, problema, er — Sorry?" Man, I needed that Spanish class. I wasn't off to a very good start.

The guy scratched his head, but he didn't appear upset. That was something. I asked, "Baños?" I was pretty sure which direction to take, but I hadn't made very many intelligent decisions that evening and didn't want to leave anything to chance.

He gasped at me. "Baños?" He said a bunch of

other words I had no idea what they were. I couldn't very well ask him for a ride back to town. I didn't know how to ask anyway. Backing out of his driveway, repeatedly apologizing, I headed down the hill in the direction he had pointed.

After stubbing my toe for the third time on the uneven rock drive, I prayed for a taxi to show up. Or a bus. Anything to get me back to Baños and civilization. A long, hot, spider-less shower would put me to rights. I would claim one of the pot scrubbers to exfoliate my skin from the chicken juice I had been obliged to sit in.

When I had reached the point where my aching toes challenged my determination to walk back to Baños, I saw two headlights turning a corner and going up the hill toward me. Please, let it be a taxi.

When it came around the corner and I saw the yellow paint, I raised my face to the heavens, exclaiming aloud, "Thank you!" for the providential gift.

The driver rolled down his window and poked his head out. It was Martin. "Jessica? What are you doing here?"

"It's a long story," I said.

"Do you need a ride?"

I climbed in, relieved he didn't ask for any explanations and that the worst of my night was done.

Martin turned around in the middle of a blind corner. With my luck, a bus would smash into us before he could find reverse. I was almost tempted to offer to drive his car for him, but he would probably consider it an insult and so I kept my mouth shut except for the exclamations which escaped me as I slammed around in the backseat.

He finally managed to get it turned around. He was the sort that needed forty acres to turn his rig around. Jamming the gear into first, we hopped forward so violently, the contents of his dashboard which had wedged themselves into the passenger corner of the dashboard, flung off. A flash of red caught my attention. I would recognize a packet of Big Red gum anywhere. I had looked all over Baños and hadn't found anyone selling my favorite gum.

"Do you like Big Red?" I asked, hoping that the ride wouldn't be so painful if I engaged Martin in conversation.

He looked at me in the rearview mirror, ignoring the road in front of him until I screamed when I thought we would plummet over the edge.

Without missing a beat, he asked, "What is Big Red?"

Opening my eyes and reassuring myself that we were still alive, I said in a squeak, "It's the cinnamon gum that just fell off your dashboard. I'd like to know where you bought it so I can get some." How could he not know what Big Red was when he must have bought it?

He didn't answer right away, thankfully paying more attention to where he pointed the front of his

Cabs, Cakes, and Corpses

car than to me. Finally, he said, "I got it from a friend."

Well that was vague. His eyes flickered to me in the backseat, and I decided that it was probably a better idea to allow him to concentrate on the road than on talking with me. His conversation was disconcerting at best.

I sat back in my seat and tried to get comfortable, but something kept whacking me on the shin. Looking down, I saw something dark wedged between the consul and the driver seat. I shoved on it, but it didn't want to budge. I moved it to the side, but that did nothing either. I considered just moving and leaving the thing be, but we went over a small precipice which made the whole car shake and it whacked once more against my throbbing shin. That would leave a gooseberry.

That was it! Pulling on the obstruction with all of my might, I lost my breath when I saw a neon yellow smiley face painted on the handle of a machete.

Chapter 25

It was Martha's missing machete. Dropping it onto the floorboard, my eyes met with Martin's in the rearview mirror and I knew I was in danger. That hadn't been just any packet of Big Red. It had been *my* pack of Big Red. The gum had been in my backpack, which he must have taken from Maria after he killed her. And the weapon he had used to kill her lay at my feet.

He held my eyes. I knew his secret. He knew I knew his secret.

"Why?" I didn't need to explain my question.

I reached down, grabbing the handle of the machete before he could. I wouldn't know how to use it without poking myself, but he didn't know that. For all he knew, I was a machete-wielding ninja warrior.

When my family sent me to Ecuador to have the adventure of a lifetime, I seriously doubted this is what they meant.

Cabs, Cakes, and Corpses

Gripping his steering wheel so hard the leather cover squeaked, Martin banged one of his hands against the dashboard. "I work harder than they do and they buy the big TV and the new car. I learn English to improve business and I save my money to buy a new car. The bank approved my loan and I was so happy, I went to Dario's bar to celebrate. Next thing I know, I wake up in the hospital and have to use down payment for my car to pay the bill. I lose the new car."

His mother must never have given him the "life is not fair" talk.

"That's no reason to kill someone, Martin," I mumbled, scared to remain silent and scared I would say the wrong thing and turn his anger on me. But hey, I was the one holding the machete.

"I tried to be nice. My car broke down one block from her house. I ask Maria for help and you know what she do? She makes fun of me. She call me lazy. She call me drunk. She call me loser. I tell her shut up but she did not listen, so I..." He sliced his finger across his throat. The gesture creeped me out worse than if he'd said the words.

"And José? Why did you kill him?" The more he talked, the slower he drove. Leaning over, I popped the lock on the passenger side door up as quickly and quietly as I could. It wasn't a very good escape plan, but it was consistent with my series of bad decisions. And it sure beat staying in the car with a psycho.

Slowing down just a little bit more, he said, "José

no drive, but he need help transporting liquor to Baños. I ask him for work, and he refused me."

Play nice, Jess. Keep Martin talking. "Why would he do that? I mean, obviously he owed you after everything he and Maria put you through."

He gunned the engine to go around the corner just as I had gotten into a crouch position to jump out of the door. We drifted over the dirt and stone road as he swerved the car out of the way of an oncoming vehicle. I couldn't see the vehicle very well, but I prayed it was Vasquez coming for me.

Martin got some control over his car and I saw my chance. Kicking the door open, I flung the machete out of the open door and I leapt out hoping to land in a tuft of soft grass. I landed in a puddle of mud. My dreams of being a stunt woman effectively crushed, I crawled over the side grateful all of my limbs worked.

Up the road I saw what I could now clearly identify as Agent Vasquez's rig as it twirled around in a perfect Rockford. The backseat window rolled down and Abuelita yelled at me, "Get in!"

Scrambling to my feet, I had the sense of mind to grab the machete glinting in the moonlight on the side of the road and hobbled over to him with one sandal on and the other one lost.

He stepped on the gas before I had even closed my door.

Tia Rosa asked, "You okay?"

I was too shocked to know if I was okay or not.

Cabs, Cakes, and Corpses

That paled in comparison to what I knew. "It was Martin!"

"I gathered as much," he said, his eyes never leaving the road as he accelerated.

My body shook so hard with adrenaline, I had a hard time buckling my seatbelt. "I got a confession and everything."

In a low growl, he said, "Of course you did."

He flashed his lights at the taxi, but Martin did not slow down. He lurched forward just as we reached the highway. Agent Vasquez braked so hard, my seatbelt locked. Ouch! I hated to think of how many bruises I would find on my person in the morning.

Martin made it across one lane of traffic, but he got no further than that. He slammed into the back of a truck hauling two cows and a horse, crunching the front of his car like an accordion and sending a poof of dark smoke into the night sky.

Agent Vasquez hopped out of his SUV, pointing at me. "Stay here," he demanded.

I still trembled so hard, I didn't think I could've moved had I wanted to. The inside of his car felt safe. I put the machete on the floorboard before I cut myself with it.

Abuelita and Tia Rosa scooted forward and they each took one of my hands, stroking them until my shaking calmed. No wonder cats liked to be pet.

"How did you know to come here?" I asked.

"Street girl run to restaurant and tell us when you call."

Tia Rosa grimaced at her sister. "You try throw her out."

"I no allow riffraff in restaurant."

"She not riffraff. She save Jessica." Tia Rosa narrowed her enormous eyes in a blistering glare at Abuelita.

I vowed to learn that little girl's name to thank her and buy an entire box of her mints. "I want to buy her lunch."

Abuelita reacted instantly. "No! First you have Lady. And now, you want little girl. Is no good!"

"We'll see about that," I said, changing the subject to avoid a fight I didn't have the strength for. The adrenaline was wearing off and an overwhelming exhaustion took over my body. "How did you convince Agent Vasquez to let you come with him?"

Tia Rosa said, "We no give him choice. We climb in car before he say 'no'."

Abuelita patted my hand. "You in trouble. We come."

I squeezed their hands while I still could, then let go to settle into the worn, leather seat to observe the scene before us. Several police cars with their sirens screaming and lights flashing surrounded Martin and his car.

In a matter of seconds, the resentful taxi driver was escorted to the back of a police car, handcuffs holding his arms behind his back.

The police got traffic moving again in no time, getting the truck off the road as well as the totaled

Cabs, Cakes, and Corpses

taxi. The animals were unharmed, but made their displeasure known by leaving steaming heaps of manure on the hood of Martin's car.

Agent Vasquez came back to his vehicle with a plastic bag. He opened it up to me and I dropped the machete into it. Without a word, he turned around and gave it to one of the policemen waiting behind him.

He got back into the car and the engine rumbled to life as he turned the ignition.

"What happens now?" I asked.

"Martin is being taken to Ambato to await his trial in jail. I'll need to get your statement tonight while it's still fresh in your mind."

I sighed. All I wanted was a hot shower and my comfortable bed.

"But first," he held his hand out to me, "you owe me five bucks."

I looked at him questioningly.

He raised his eyebrows and looked over at me. "That is, unless you want to go to jail tonight too for shoplifting."

The chocolate and powdered sugar! I'd forgotten all about that. It must still be in the back of the pickup with all the dead chickens.

Agent Vasquez chuckled. "Don't worry about it, Jessica. You make me a batch of your famous goofballs, and we'll call it even."

"How'd you hear about those?"

He smiled. "Abuelita and Tia Rosa argued over

which was better before the little girl told us what had happened to you. Your goofballs or your doughnuts."

"The fried balls," voiced Abuelita.

"The doughnuts," countered Tia Rosa.

Agent Vasquez raised his hand for silence. "But first, we must get you into a shower. I can't interview you with that stench and I doubt Sylvia will want you in her restaurant in your current state. You stink."

Oh, and I knew it. If only my family could see me now. Shoplifter. Detective. Stowaway. Heartbreaker … The list got longer the more I thought about it. The past week had been the stuff of novels, which gave me an idea….

"May I borrow a piece of paper and a pen?" I asked.

Pulling out a notepad from his pocket, Agent Vasquez tore out a page toward the back and clicked his pen as he handed it to me.

In the five-minute drive back to Sylvia's restaurant, I scribbled out an outline. I had a feeling about this one. I had started and stopped dozens of comics (Come on, I'm a web developer and graphic designer, not a novelist). I felt a bit like Joan Wilder in Romancing the Stone, but if it worked for her, why not me too? Just change the genre from romance to mystery … or adventure … with a touch of chick lit and comedy. My family would love it. They'd be happy I was drawing again.

Agent Vasquez looked at me funny, but he didn't ask.

Cabs, Cakes, and Corpses

I was too gross to walk through the restaurant, so we went through the side door, past a very happy Lady, and into the kitchen through the screen door.

I had no sooner entered the room than I was bowled over by Sylvia and Adi. Abuelita and Tia Rosa would not be outdone by the younger members of their family and I soon found myself surrounded by friends, all of them jockeying for the best hugging position. Abuelita used her bony elbows and Adi used her superior height to advantage. None of them complained that I was dirty and smelled like deceased poultry. I stood as close to the roses Christian had sent over as I could. Poor guy. I was so convinced he'd done it, I'd acted like a complete idiot to avoid him. On the other hand, maybe he'd leave me alone if he thought I was crazy.

Like she could read my thoughts, Adi said, "Christian was flattered you thought he was an edgy bad boy. You're not going to get rid of him easily."

I rolled my eyes. "Of course he'd like that."

And then the questions came. Agent Vasquez poured coffee for everyone in a ring around the island as I related everything that had transpired between the time I had last seen them until that moment. Agent Vasquez soon took over the questions, frantically jotting down every detail I shared in his notepad. I was grateful I wouldn't have to relate the story again. But there were some details I didn't understand.

"How come we didn't suspect Martin? Did you

check his alibi? And how did he murder Maria without being seen by Christian or Dario?"

Agent Vasquez scowled. "I had one of my lieutenants check his alibi. Martin said he'd gone to the store on the corner of the alleyway to buy beer for the guys at the auto shop. The storekeeper and the mechanics confirmed his story. He had to have done it then. That he did it quickly is evidenced by how Dario found Maria. She was in her car with the engine running. When I took Dario's statement, he told me he'd waved to Martin on his way up the alleyway. He was close enough to the store, we assumed he was only buying beer."

"What about the machete? He took it with him. Didn't anyone notice?"

"Until I read through his confession and talk to him myself, I can't know for sure, but hadn't you asked Maria to return your backpack? If she was on her way to you, your bag would have been in her car and Martin could have used it to hide the machete and stow it somewhere until he could hide it."

"That explains why my Big Red was in his car. I hope he didn't get rid of my e-reader."

"I'll find out."

I was exhausted and I desperately needed a shower. My skin felt grimy with the fine film of dried mud covering my arms and legs. At least, I hoped it was just dirt.

When every detail had been recounted to the best of my memory, and Agent Vasquez had tucked his notepad back in his pocket, Sylvia wrapped her arms around me in an all-consuming embrace. She squeezed me so tightly, she pushed all the air out of my lungs and I couldn't breathe. But it felt so nice.

The coffee got me through a teary call with Fernanda — who promised to swing by for lunch before school tomorrow — my much anticipated shower, and into my pajamas. After that, I didn't remember anything until my alarm went off the next morning at the good, decent hour of eight o'clock. I stretched and relaxed in my comfy bed, finally feeling like I was on vacation.

Chapter 26

One week later, we were able to lure Agent Vasquez away from Ambato and the mountain of paperwork he complained about. As with everything in this country, it could be dealt with mañana. My doughnuts, however, tasted best when eaten fresh. Five dozen golden doughnuts cooled on wire racks, spread out over the center table with bowls of frosting and sprinkles ready to decorate them.

My laptop was ready too. It was my family's night to call and I thought they'd want to see everyone. The comic I'd sent them yesterday had already received several replies. They praised my creativity and imagination. They thought I'd made it all up.

I mixed up the goofball batter while Abuelita and Tia Rosa fought over who would be in charge of frying them.

"You burn balls," charged Abuelita.

"You sabotage! You turn burner high and make oil too hot," fired back Tia Rosa.

Jake was home from his jungle excursion, looking as tanned and muscled as ever. An embarrassing urge to giggle every time he looked at me had me focusing intently on the batter in front of me as I whipped it into submission. Better that the goofballs turn out as hard as rocks than embarrass myself by acting half my age. Abuelita would notice and she would torment me about it. Or worse — she would tell Jake.

Sylvia and Adriana were busy over the stove, making a typical dish they said I would love. We had a lot to celebrate. A murderer had been caught, Jake was home, my family was calling, Adi's bridesmaid gowns had been approved by the bride and she had her first real commission, my doughnuts looked perfect ... Oh, and Agent Vasquez ended up being a pretty cool guy. (I think he had an eye for Sylvia. If he was willing to brave Abuelita, then he forever had my respect.) I'd even caught Abuelita calling him by his first name, Washington. When Adi called him Washo, he had seemed pleased. He'd been so busy tying up all the loose ends in the Guzmán's double murder case, we hadn't seen him since the night of Martin's arrest.

"Whatever happened to Martha and her pack of kids?" asked Washo as he sipped on a glass of tree tomato juice. (Which, I found out does not taste like tomatoes in the least.)

Sylvia topped off his glass. "Maria willed everything to Martha. The house, the car, everything. You can imagine, she doesn't want to live in the house or drive the car, but she can sell them for a good price. The money will really help her."

Abuelita chimed in. "Maria better sister dead. She terrible mean alive."

Tia Rosa poked her with the fork she used to turn the goofballs over in the hot oil. "Is not nice speak bad of dead person, okay?"

Abuelita shrugged her bony shoulders. "She mean."

Another stab. "And what people say about you? Hmm?"

Ignoring them, Washo said, "I drove by The Lava Lounge on my way here. Dario had big signs up announcing a reopening party."

"He is one cool customer. I couldn't understand everything he said on the news, but he didn't look worried at all when he was shut down." I have little respect for people ... well, little was too much ... I had *no* respect for people who cut corners and deceived others just to make a quick buck. I had rejoiced when he'd been shut down for selling counterfeit liquor.

Sylvia agreed. "Take comfort in the small fortune he must have spent on fines and bribes. Maybe the hit to his wallet will teach him a lesson."

Adi grinned at me. "Unfortunately for you, Christian came out smelling like a rose. He was under investigation on the suspicion of being an illegal liquor provider, but it turns out he really is a legal importer. Dario just did business with Maria and José because they could offer what he claims is the same goods for much cheaper. Christian thinks he's pretty hot stuff for being on the news."

He'd been so busy being a media star, he'd pretty much left me alone. I did manage to apologize to him for acting like a lunatic at our last meeting, but that had ended badly. He tried to kiss me and I punched him in the nose. Not having grown up with brothers, I have no idea where that had come from. I swear I'm not a violent person.

I checked my watch. I could just imagine Mammy and my sisters crowding into Mom and Dad's house, each fighting to get a better spot in front of the camera. They had a lot more in common with Abuelita and Tia Rosa than I had believed possible.

Mixing the chocolate and powdered sugar until it was smooth and creamy, I placed the bowl in front of Washo. I didn't trust Abuelita not to lick the chocolate out of the bowl before the goofballs were fried and cool enough to handle.

I grabbed a piece of chorizo from the plate by Adi and whistled for Lady. She met me at the screen door, took her prize gently in her mouth, and trotted back up the stairs to her post. Ten days had passed and nobody had called to claim her. She seemed perfectly content where she was and Abuelita slipped her food when she thought no one was looking.

Jake sat by Washo and started dipping the goofballs. "Are you going to tell your folks about your upcoming plans?" he asked me.

"Absolutely! I can't thank you and Adi enough for arranging a special tour for me." They'd thought of everything. Knowing I loved to ride bikes, they'd planned a ride from Baños to Puyo, stopping along the way to take the cable cars across the river to see the waterfalls. Once in Puyo, we'd go to the Animal Rescue Center. It was like a jungle zoo for injured and endangered animals.

From Puyo, we'd go deeper into the jungle to a place called Tena (at which point, Adi would leave us to do the final fittings for the wedding party). Jake had arranged for some friends of his to take us whitewater rafting on the Rio Napo. And then, to top everything off, we'd go to Misahualli where the pesky monkeys stole water bottles, sunglasses, and cameras. We'd hike a waterfall trail, visit a butterfly farm, and take a canoe up the river to a cacao plantation where we could make our own chocolate. We would leave in two days.

My computer chimed and we huddled around the screen, squeezing and pushing just like my family did thousands of miles away. Only Washo stayed on the other side of the table, saying that he didn't want to interfere. I didn't insist. After tonight, we'd most likely see less of him anyway.

Mom and Sylvia squealed together and complimented each other's hair while Abuelita chewed Dad out for letting his silver hair grow too long. Tia Rosa thought it looked beautiful, which probably did more to convince Dad to visit the barber shop than Abuelita's criticism.

Kids were introduced and I felt my jaw clench when I saw Jessamyn notice Jake. She flipped her perfectly smooth locks over her shoulder and crossed her slender legs. He made my night when he chose the moment she flashed her brightest smile to rest his hand on my shoulder. It could have been a brotherly gesture, but I gloried in the one and only time in my memory when a boy showed more attention to me than to my younger, prettier sister. It's the little things.

"We loved your comic, honey," Mammy said. "How did you think of all of that?"

Abuelita answered before I could. "She do it."

Tia Rosa shoved her glasses up her nose. "All of it. Jessica great driver."

That revelation was met with a lengthy silence.

Mom finally found her voice. "The corpse in the cab? The bootleg booze? The machete murder? That all happened?"

Mammy pumped her fist in the air. "Woo hoo! My Jess solved a murder case! I knew you had it in you, pumpkin. I hope you took a lot of pictures."

Jessenia whipped out her cell phone and poked at the screen while keeping Jayden's fingers away from the computer's camera. "You can't stay there. It's too dangerous. There's a flight leaving first thing in the morning. You'd have three layovers, but it's the quickest way out of there. Hang on a moment. I'll call."

"No, Jessenia. I want to stay. Despite all the problems, I'm having the time of my life and I'm not ready to come home yet."

I must have spoken firmly enough. She lowered her phone and pulled Jayden closer to her. I wiggled my fingers and made a funny face at him.

Dad, who hadn't said anything since Abuelita and Tia Rosa had outed my secret, said, "We did send you to Baños for an adventure. You've always been an overachiever and I'm proud of you."

"Just try to be more careful, will you, Jess?" added Mom.

"I will. I don't plan on being involved in any more murder investigations ever again."

That got me a thumbs up from Washo.

Right then, we lost our Internet signal, but it had been good while it had lasted. I missed my family, but they seemed to be managing fine without me. I'd write them a long email later. With a sigh, I pushed the screen down and moved my laptop out of the way to make room for the sugary treats covering the island.

"I heard what you said, Jessica, and I'm holding you to it. No more murder investigations," Washo said with a smile.

As if that was necessary! I mean, what are the chances, right?

Raising my hand in a solemn promise, I said, "I

certainly don't plan on it, but if anyone happens to die in my presence, I promise you will be the first person I call."

We all laughed at the ridiculousness of it. Seriously, what are the odds?

Thank you!

Thank you for reading *Cabs, Cakes, and Corpses*. I hope you enjoyed it. I'd love to know what you thought of Jessica's adventure, so please leave a review. I read all of them!

If you would like to know when my next book is available, you can:
* sign up for my New Release newsletter. I only send out a newsletter to announce a new release. No spam!
* follow me on twitter at @BeccaBloomWrite
* friend my Facebook page at @BeccaBloomWrites

Seco de Pollo

Prep Time: 20 minutes

Cook Time: 1 hour, 30 minutes (6-8 in a slow cooker)

Yield: For 8 people

Seco de pollo is the first meal Jessica enjoyed on arriving to Ecuador at Abuelita's Kitchen. It's best described as chicken in a stewed sauce and is a typical dish enjoyed all over Ecuador. Jess thought it was delicious and I think you will too!

Ingredients:

- 8 pieces of chicken (thigh, breast… whichever you prefer)
- 2 teaspoons of ground cumin
- 2 tsp ground paprika (In Ecuador, we use achiote seeds or ground achiote. If you

Seco de Pollo

have that, great! If not, paprika works just as well.)
- 2-3 tablespoons of oil
- 1 onion, quartered
- 6-8 garlic cloves
- 1 to 2 cups of beer (Pilsener is the beer of choice here, but any light/mild flavor will do. You can substitute chicken broth if you prefer.)
- 1 cup of orange juice
- 4-6 tomatoes (1 pound), quartered
- 2 bell peppers, seeds removed and cut into chunks
- 1 bunch cilantro, save some to add at the end
- 1 bunch parsley leaves, save some to chop finely and add at the end
- 2 tsp dry oregano or 2-3 fresh oregano sprigs
- Salt and pepper to taste

Instructions:

1. Heat the oil and brown the chicken.
2. Blend together: paprika, cumin, salt, pepper, onion, garlic, beer, orange juice, tomatoes, bell peppers, cilantro, parsley, and oregano until smooth.
3. Pour the blended mixture over the chicken. Bring to a boil.

Seco de Pollo

4. Reduce the heat and cook on low heat for about an hour.

*If the chicken is cooked, but sauce isn't thick yet, remove the chicken pieces, turn the heat to high and cook the sauce until it thickens (10-15 minutes).

*Once the chicken is cooked, taste the sauce to adjust salt/spices. If the flavor is slightly bitter from the beer, just add some freshly squeezed orange juice/lemon juice.

5. Once the sauce has thickened, add the chicken pieces back to the pot.

6. Serve over white rice.

Time-Saving Tip: Use a slow cooker! Put the uncooked chicken pieces and blended mixture in the slow cooker for 6-8 hours. The sauce will need thickening, so just follow the notes in step 4 until you get your desired consistency. This recipe is very forgiving, so feel free to adjust according to your taste.

Mammy's Goofballs

Prep Time: 10 minutes for the dough and frosting
  Cook Time: about 3 minutes per goofball
  Yield: 30-40 (If you're anything like me, you never get the same amount twice!)

This treat is perfect for satisfying a doughnut craving when you don't feel like leaving home. Warning: It's almost impossible to stop after one. Make sure you're not alone in the room with them!

Dough Ingredients:

- 2 cups flour
- 1/4 cup sugar
- 1 tablespoon baking powder
- 1 teaspoon salt
- 1 teaspoon cinnamon or nutmeg (If you can't decide, use a dash of both. I do.)

Mammy's Goofballs

- 1/4 cup oil
- 3/4 cup milk
- 1 egg
- Oil for frying (approx. 1-1 1/2 cups)

Frosting Ingredients:

- 1/2 square unsweetened chocolate (4oz)
- 1/4 teaspoon vanilla
- 1 1/4 cup powdered sugar
- 2 tablespoons milk

Instructions:

1. Mix together: all listed ingredients *except* for the frying oil. The dough should be slightly sticky.
2. Heat the oil to 350°F (or until the dough sizzles when it's dropped in). While you can deep fry, it's not necessary so long as half the ball is covered with oil.
3. Make teaspoon-size balls and scrape them off the spoon into the preheated frying oil. They'll look small, but they grow as they fry.
4. Fry until golden brown (about 1 1/2 minutes) and flip them over to the other side for the same amount of time or until golden brown.
5. Melt the chocolate in the microwave or a small saucepan and mix it with all the frosting ingredients.
6. Dip the goofballs in the frosting while they're still warm.
7. Enjoy! Buen provecho!

About the Author

Becca Bloom is a budding detective, inquisitive world traveler, developing storyteller, and blossoming cozy mystery writer.

She loves happy endings and laughter and does her best to include both in her novels.

Other Books by Becca Bloom

Cabs, Cakes, and Corpses: Murder on the Equator, Book 1

Rum Raisin Revenge: Murder on the Equator, Book 2

Cold Case Crumble: Murder on the Equator, Book 3

Diamonds and Donuts: Murder on the Equator, Book 4

Chocolate Cherry Cheater: Murder on the Equator, Book 5

Made in the USA
Columbia, SC
01 December 2023